The Golden Seed

A magical blend of two realities

Orest Stocco

The Golden Seed

ISBN 978-1-926442-00-6

Edited by Penny Lynn Cates

Cover Design by Penny Lynn Cates

Penny Lynn, my golden seed,
this one's for you.

Table of Contents

1. Elmer Coventry

Elmer Coventry was just a cranky old man. Or so Jordan thought until he said something that cranky old men simply don't say: "Until you resolve the conflict in your heart you will never find the peace you're looking for."

Taken aback by this strange comment, which was so out of context with the one-sided conversation they were having about the rumor of a casino coming to the Beach, to which Elmer objected vociferously, Jordan didn't know what to say; so he just stared at his new client with a blank look on his face. Elmer spoke again—

"Nonetheless, life's a gamble Jordan; but unlike casinos that seem to favor the odds, you can beat the game if you learn how to play by the rules."

"What game?"

"In your case, freedom."

Again Jordan stared blank-eyed. "Freedom?"

"Yes. Freedom from yourself. That's the endgame. Look, I have to go into town for groceries. I should be back before you finish."

Jordan drove his lawn tractor off his trailer and mowed Elmer's lawn, and then he took out his gas-powered weed-eater and trimmed the yard. Just as he was putting it away Elmer pulled into his driveway. Carrying a couple of plastic bags of groceries from the food market, he invited Jordan into the house.

This was the second time Jordan had done Elmer Coventry's lawn. The first time he cut it two weeks to the day, Elmer wasn't very talkative. He told Jordan what to do and left him to his work and then paid him, and Jordan went to his next job a couple of streets over little suspecting what he was getting himself into.

"Are you on a tight schedule today?" Elmer asked, as he took his groceries out of the bags to put away into his fridge and kitchen cupboards.

"I'm on my own schedule," Jordan replied, with a hint of pride in his voice.

Elmer turned and looked Jordan in the eye, and without mincing words he said, "It's important for you to be your own man, isn't it?"

Jordan grimaced. *"Where's this guy coming from?"*

"Well?" Elmer said, but Jordan didn't know what to say.

Elmer finished putting his groceries away and poured two mugs of coffee from the fresh pot he had put on before leaving the house and placed them on his round kitchen table, one on each of the two plastic yellow placemats; and then he got spoons and milk out of the fridge and sat down still waiting for Jordan to reply. The sugar was on the table, along with the salt and pepper on another placemat in the center of the table. Jordan still had no idea what to say, and he put milk and sugar into his coffee and took a sip. He wanted a cigarette badly.

"Not everyone can be their own man," Elmer volunteered, as he gently poured the milk into his coffee. "You've heard the old saying, many are called but few are chosen? Well, Jordan; you've been chosen, and I'd like to know what you're going to do about it. Are you ready to play or not?"

While mowing the lawn and trimming the edges alongside the fence and around the house and big red maple tree Jordan thought about what his client had said about the game of life, and he wondered how he could possibly know how he felt; and now he told him that he had been chosen. *"Endgame?"*

To his surprise, Jordan spoke out of character, as though compelled to tell Elmer Coventry what he felt: "I made the choice to be my own man a long time ago in my father's barn when I had to work like one of those wartime orphans for nothing but food and shelter and the clothes on my back. I've always wanted to be my own man from the day I left the farm. That's why I work for myself now."

"Life makes orphans of us all one day, Jordan; that's just the way the cookie crumbles. Many men are self-employed but aren't their own man. It's in here where it counts," Elmer said, tapping his chest with his fingers. "Not until you resolve the conflict in your heart will you ever be your own man."

Jordan was irritated now. "What makes you think I'm conflicted?"

"Aren't you?" Elmer asked, with a big smile on his wrinkled face.

Elmer's clear blue eyes twinkled, and his face lit up like a sun that filled the room with a warm glow and Jordan felt something he had not felt in a long while: love. But he had never experienced love from a stranger before. He felt it when his mother smiled at him that way, and from his wife Maria long before he was inveigled by his fellow teacher who gave him a shoulder to cry on when his wife's love no longer sustained him; and he felt disarmed by the warmth of Elmer's love.

"Yes, I am," he confessed, staring helplessly into Elmer's eyes.

"There you go, then," Elmer said, with a shrug of cold indifference that took Jordan completely by surprise. "Now, let's get to the business at hand," Elmer continued, and Jordan expected to get paid; but Elmer didn't mean that at all. He rested his arms on the table and looked Jordan in the eyes with such a powerful gaze that Jordan became lightheaded and swooned like he had been injected by a heavy dose of loving kindness, and the earth dropped away from under his feet and he was floating on air. *"Are you ready?"* he heard Elmer's voice, as if from a great distance. *"Are you ready this time, Jordan?"*

"Ready?" Jordan asked, snapping out of his daze. "Ready for what?"

"What else? To play the endgame, of course," Elmer said.

"What endgame?" Jordan asked, suddenly spooked by the strange man.

Elmer Coventry was just a little over five feet tall and not more than a hundred and forty pounds, so his size didn't threaten Jordan; Jordan was spooked by what he had just experienced and this endgame that he was asked to play. He took a mouthful of coffee and forced himself to look into Elmer's eyes.

But he felt it again, and every fiber of his being tried to resist the love that poured out of Elmer's eyes that awakened feelings he had been holding back since childhood, and he felt like he was in the center of a cyclone swirling in painful memories and he swooned in a dizzy spell that forced him to rest his arms on the kitchen table and hold his head in his hands to keep from fainting.

Elmer waited for Jordan to collect himself. A minute or so later Jordan took his hands away from his face. "I'm sorry. I don't know what got over me. I must have caught a bug or something. You were saying something—"

"I was saying that it's time you took the bull by the horns and get on with what you were called by God to do—"

"*What?*" Jordan squealed instinctively like an animal caught in a steel trap and jumped to his feet. "*What are you, some kind of religious nut or something?*"

"What I am Jordan is your answer to a very old question," Elmer replied, with a stern look in his clear blue eyes. "Sit down and stop making a fool of yourself. Do I look like a nut? How long have you been looking for an answer to your dilemma? How long must you go on pretending you've got the world by the proverbial short hairs? You think you're your own man, but you're fooling no-one but yourself. You know in here that you're just as much a slave as everyone else. Give it up, Jordan. You have to decide now what you want out of life. You can't put it off any longer. You've been called to a higher purpose, and if you don't heed the call you're going to suffer like you've never suffered in any of your former lives. Here's your payment for today; and when you come back in two weeks let me know if you want to play the endgame and we can take it from there. Fair enough?"

Jordan was speechless. He reached over and picked up the small bills from the table, but he was too stunned to count them as he normally would and put them into his pocket. "I'll get you a receipt," he said, not knowing what else to say, and he went out to his truck for his receipt book. He wrote one up and gave it to Elmer who had followed him outside with a curious smile on his wrinkled face.

"I'll see you in two weeks," Elmer said.

"Yeah, sure," Jordan stammered, and drove off completely mystified by the man whom Elmer's neighbor called a cranky old curmudgeon.

2. The Master's Gaze

"What higher purpose?" Jordan asked himself, as he cut Mrs. Cummings' lawn. "Called by God? I don't believe in God. He's crazy. He's just a crazy old man. There is no God. There is no higher purpose. *This is it, old man!*"

But try as he may, Jordan could not get that look out of his mind. Just thinking about the love that poured out of Elmer's eyes made him dizzy again, and he had to shut down the lawn tractor to get his bearings.

Mrs. Cummings walked over. "Are you all right, Jordan?"

"What? Oh, it's you Mrs. Cummings."

"Are you all right? You've been sitting here for half an hour."

"Have I? Half an hour? No way."

"Yes. Is everything all right? Are you feeling okay?"

"I'm fine. I was just taking a break."

"Are you sure? You look a little pale."

"I'm fine, Mrs. Cummings. I should be finished in an hour."

"As long as you're feeling okay," the recently widowed Mrs. Cummings said, with a worried look on her kind elderly face.

"Thank you for asking," Jordan said, and resumed mowing the lawn. When he finished he drove his tractor back onto his trailer and took out his weed eater and did around the yard and flower gardens. Mrs. Cummings had his cheque ready.

"Would you like a cold drink, Jordan?" she asked.

"No thank you," he said, handing her the receipt. "I'll be back in two weeks. It may be Friday though, Mrs. Cummings. I may have a long day Thursday because I picked up a few more customers over the weekend."

"That's fine. If I'm not here, I'll leave the cheque on the table. You're doing a fine job, Jordan. Thank you."

"You're welcome," he said, and went to his next job stopping at McDonald's on his way to pick up a coffee and muffin. He preferred Tim Hortons, but for a dollar thirty-nine special Jordan got his coffee and a muffin at McDonald's. *"Take care of the pennies and the dollars will take care of themselves,"* his father used to say.

This was his second year in Hampton Beach, simply called the Beach, and he was doing much better than he anticipated. When he started *Jordan's Lawn and Property Management Service* he didn't know how he was going to do; but he posted an ad in the local paper and went all over town posting flyers, offering a discount to new customers, and in less than two months he picked up forty-eight clients for lawn service that included leaf removal in the fall and a dozen homes to look after for snowbirds that went south for the winter. He kept their driveways clean and checked their homes weekly, and within a year he had enough winter and summer customers to relieve his fear of failing; and he even felt comfortable enough the second year to buy the two bedroom bungalow that he was leasing.

He could have kept teaching and retired with a full pension at fifty-five and not have to worry for the rest of his life, but he couldn't stomach his life any longer; so when the school term ended he resigned his position and left his wife Sharon and moved back to Ontario which he loved far more than Manitoba which he hated as much as he hated the prairie province of Saskatchewan where he was born.

He pulled into John Maynard's yard and smoked a cigarette before starting his lawn. John was a bank manager from Toronto who came to his cottage in the Beach with his wife and family every third or fourth weekend, but they never stayed more than a few days; and as Jordan rode his tractor he thought of Elmer and the gaze that he could not get out of his mind, and it still spooked him.

Something happened to Jordan while mowing Mrs. Cummings' lawn that spooked him even more. While sitting on his tractor he had an experience that shook the very foundations of his normal, albeit troubled life: he left his body. But he wasn't alone. Elmer Coventry was with him. Elmer took him by the arm and lifted him out of his body and zoomed him off to another world.

They lighted like two birds on the grounds of an ancient Greek-like temple that glowed in the light of a brilliant white city that was like no city Jordan had ever seen before in real life or the movies. "Where are we?" he asked, starring in amazement.

"The spiritual city of Agam Des," replied Elmer.

"What are we doing here?" Jordan asked.

"Come with me," Elmer said, and they walked to the front of the temple. Three wide low steps at the front of the temple led to an alcove underneath a marble arch, and just beyond stood a lectern with an open book that glowed in a golden light that gave Jordan the feeling that all the wisdom of the world poured out of the book, and he stared transfixed; and then Elmer put his hand on his shoulder. "What does that say?" he asked, pointing to the large marble archway. But Jordan didn't recognize the letters that looked like ancient hieroglyphic writing.

As he stared at the strange writing a great weight descended upon him because the writing became clear: "Do not enter unless you have been invited." Jordan felt a desperate need to enter the Temple of Golden Wisdom, but he knew he wasn't allowed; and a great sorrow filled his heart.

Suddenly he was filled with grace and his sadness disappeared. His whole being was awash in the same sweet love that he felt at Elmer's house, and he wanted to break down and cry. Then a bald man in a white robe appeared from one side of the alcove and walked up to Elmer and Jordan. He eyes were as electric as Elmer's were when he gazed at him in his kitchen, and love flowed out of the man's eyes in no less abundance; and Jordan was filled with so much goodness it made him tremble.

"You are not ready yet to read the Holy Book of Gnostic Wisdom," said the Gnostic Master who was the appointed guardian of the temple. His voice sounded like it came from a deep cavern and bounced off the walls of Jordan's mind like an echo. "To enter, you must die before you die," said the Master. "That is the price one must pay to live the Gnostic Way, if one chooses to play the final game of life."

"The endgame?" Jordan said, looking at Elmer.

"Yes," said the Gnostic Master, with a loving smile.

Elmer embraced the temple guardian before parting, and then he put his arm around Jordan's shoulder and they walked down the steps and Jordan heard Mrs. Cummings asking if he was alright, but he was too stunned to know what to say.

When he finished doing the banker's lawn Jordan drove to Elmer's house and knocked on his door. "What the hell do you want?' Elmer asked.

"Pardon?" Jordan said, surprised by Elmer's manner.

"You got your money, didn't you?' Elmer spit out, with a suspicious look.

"Yes," Jordan said, dumbfounded by Elmer's change of character.

"Then what the hell are you doing back here?" Elmer asked.

"I wanted to talk," Jordan stammered.

"About what? The casino? I don't give a damn what they do in this stupid town. If it's not one thing it's another. It's the same old story. Money money money! They never get enough! They're all a bunch of money-mooching retards looking for a cheap buck! That's what we've come down to in this trashcan world of ours. It's fast becoming a refuse dump of lost souls and I don't know why I even bother!"

Stunned, Jordan didn't know what to say. Elmer looked at him with the most foul and bitter scowl that he had ever seen and slammed the door in his face, and Jordan left more confused than he'd ever been in his entire life.

"*What's happening to me?*" he asked, as he drove to his next customer; but he was too shaken up to work and went home for a stiff shot of rye.

3. A World of Confusion

Jordan couldn't fall asleep. He kept thinking of his experience with Elmer in the strange city of Agam Des. *"Was I hallucinating?"*

He lit another cigarette. Jordan started smoking again the year before moving to the Beach in Georgian Bay, Ontario. He had been off cigarettes from the day he was challenged by the science teacher in the staff room in Regency High School in Winnipeg where he taught English Literature. "Put up or shut up, Jordan," science teacher Mike Stafford said to Jordan in front of all the teachers.

Mike was in training to run his third Manitoba Marathon, and the way he went on about his training schedule finally got to Jordan—

"Why are you making such a big deal of running a marathon? Anyone can run a marathon if they train for it. Even me," he said, with surprising bravado that he knew the moment it left his mouth he would regret saying.

"You're all talk, Jordan. The way you smoke your lungs couldn't take the training. I know how hard it is, and I've never smoked a day in my life!"

Some teachers laughed, embarrassing Jordan. He had opened a door he didn't want to enter and didn't know how to close it without losing respect.

"I'm sure if he puts his mind to it he can run the Manitoba Marathon," Sharon Henderson, an unhappy unmarried History teacher said in Jordan's defense.

"I doubt it," Eric Tobin, the beer-bellied Geography teacher replied. "Mike's right. His lungs couldn't take the training. Stick to golf, Jordan."

Jordan knew what he would have to sacrifice to save face, so he bit his tongue and suffered the humiliation in bitter silence.

The following Monday Mike related his experience of running twenty miles on Sunday, his second longest run before the marathon. "But it's the last six miles and three hundred and eighty-five yards that count. That's what makes or breaks you. I think I can break four hours this year. That's what I'm shooting for."

Jordan bit his tongue. He poured a coffee and sat down beside Sharon and took out his cigarettes. Sharon took a puff on her cigarette and whispered into Jordan's ear, "I wish he'd put a sock in it."

Jordan smiled and flicked his lighter to light his cigarette.

"Another nail for your coffin, eh Jordan?" Mike said, and snickered.

"We all have to die someday, Mike; so why not get the most out of life while you can?" Jordan said, and took a long satisfying drag.

"You think you're getting the most out of life by smoking? What a joke!" Mike said, deliberately provoking Jordan, who rubbed Mike the wrong way from the day Jordan replaced his friend and fellow teacher who committed suicide.

"What's that supposed to mean?" Jordan shot back.

"Quality of life, Jordan. You have no idea what getting the most out of life means until you've experienced the runner's high. It's even better than sex!"

The game was on, and it was Jordan's move; but he didn't have a comeback. He took another drag on his cigarette, and said, "I've never experienced a runner's high, Mike; but I've had moments on the golf course that I would compare to great sex any day of the week—"

"*Compare?* There's no comparison with the runner's high! It's a whole new world of satisfaction. Nothing can compare to the runner's high! When you run across that finish line you feel like you've just conquered Everest, and how many people do you know that have conquered Everest?"

"Are you comparing a marathon to climbing Mount Everest?"

"I'm saying that running a marathon is an accomplishment that very few people will ever experience, and you're not one of them."

"I don't believe that," Sharon said, jumping to Jordan's defense again.

"I'd bet a thousand bucks he can't run the Manitoba Marathon!"

Whether it was some primal alpha instinct or pure ego, Jordan reacted with the swiftness of a cornered animal—*"I'll take that bet!"* Everyone froze. The gauntlet had been thrown. "A thousand bucks says I can run next year's Manitoba Marathon!"

Mike walked over to Jordan and stuck out his hand. Jordan grabbed it and shook firmly. "You're all witnesses," Mike said.

"I'm putting my money on Jordan," Sharon said.

"How much?" Mike asked.

"A hundred bucks," Sharon said.

"You're on," Mike said, and gave her his hand to shake. "Anyone else?"

Mrs. Brumby was tempted, but no one else backed Jordan; which only gave him more fuel for his fire. "So where can I get a good pair of runners, Mike?" Jordan asked, now that he had his respect back and felt more alive than he had in years.

"PHEIDIPPIDES store downtown. You can get everything you need for running there. Good luck, Jordan. You're going to need it."

"I don't believe in luck, Mike. I believe in myself," Jordan replied. Even his voice was different now. His adrenalin was pumping.

"Then we'll see what you're really made of," Mike shot back.

"An easy grand," Jordan replied, and after school he drove straight to PHEIDIPPIDES and had a talk with the store manager, who was himself a marathon runner, and then he bought a pair of Nike runners and running togs for summer and winter, and several books on running that the owner highly recommended, one by the champion runner Frank Shorter, and he read late into the night on the best training methods for running a marathon; but first he had to quit smoking, and he read until he ran out of cigarettes, savoring every puff as if it was his last.

It cost Jordan all the egoic will that he could muster, and more; but it was worth it to watch Mike eat crow in front of their fellow teachers when he ran his first Manitoba Marathon, which Sharon recorded with the photograph of Mike handing Jordan his cheque that she framed and hung in the staff room to memorialize Jordan's victory and Mike's humiliation, and Jordan ran two more provincial marathons as well as the iconic Boston Marathon before his knees gave out and he had to stop running altogether and he took up golfing with the same passionate commitment; and he started smoking again the year before resigning his position and walking out on his wife and moving to Hampton Beach where he and Sharon had stopped for the day to enjoy the sandy shores of Georgian Bay on their way to Peggy's Cove Newfoundland where they were going for their honeymoon.

Jordan had honeymooned in Peggy's Cove with his first wife Maria, but he told Sharon that they had honeymooned in Victoria, British Columbia instead, and their ill-founded marriage began to seriously fall apart the following year when his new student Jason Michaels who had transferred from Alberta humiliated him in front of his class and forced him to see that his life was a lie like the fallen hero in Camus' novel *The Fall* that he assigned to his senior's reading list every year, and he walked away from his second marriage with even less consideration than he had for his first wife Maria and their son Mark and daughter Lisa.

"It was cold-blooded," Genaro, Maria's brother and father of four, reacted to the way Jordan had walked out on his wife and children, shaking his head in disgust. "That fucking *mangiacake* didn't have a pot to piss in and we took him into the family like one of our own, and that's how he treated you? It makes me sick!"

No-one saw it coming, least of all Maria; but Jordan had put all of that behind him, and as he sat at his kitchen table in the Beach smoking one cigarette after another and drinking one beer after another his whole life swirled around him like a storm of confused emotions, and he blamed it all on his strange new client Elmer Coventry. *"I don't know what the hell he did to me, but he did something..."*

4. The Humiliation

Like everything he couldn't explain rationally (God, spirits, and things that went bump in the night), and everything that he refused to see about himself (vanity, false pride, and self-deception), Jordan cavalierly dismissed or repressed to the recesses of his mind; and his unconscious was full of unresolved thoughts and feelings that came spewing out when he met the strange man Elmer Coventry.

It was as though Elmer had spiked his coffee with a mind-altering drug like the jungle brew the Amazonian shamans called *ayahuasca* that altered his consciousness and released all of his repressed thoughts and feelings that gave life to his demons, but he didn't do drugs; the closest he came to doing drugs was the pot he smoked once with his son Mark who wanted nothing more to do with his father after he walked out on his wife and family and moved in with his lover Sharon.

"You're a selfish bastard," Mark spit out at him, when his father tried to explain why he left his mother for the other woman. "You betrayed us, Dad; and I hate you. I'll never speak to you again as long as I live. You mean nothing to me. *Nothing!*"

Jordan tried to reach out to his son over the next year, giving him plenty of time to come to terms with what he refused to call a betrayal; but his son wouldn't hear of it. "He betrayed us, Mom; and I can't forgive him for what he did to us. I can't. You know why? Because my whole life he told me to be honest and true to myself. Well I'm honest and true to myself, and I hate him. He's the one that's false. He betrayed us, Mom; and I can't forgive him. *I can't!*"

"Mark, he's your father—"

"He conceived me, but I don't know who that man is who betrayed us. He's a stranger to me, Mom. He's not my father. *He's not, Mom!*"

"I don't know who he is either, Mom," Mark's sister replied.

"Lisa, I don't know who he is either; but he's still your father whether we like it or not. I know he hurt us, but we have to get on with our life—"

"I know we do, but I can't forgive him," Mark said, fighting back his anger. "I can't explain it, but if I forgive him it's like condoning his betrayal; and I can't do that. I'm sorry, Mom. I want nothing do with him. *Nothing!*"

His sister Lisa did patch things up with her father, as much as they could be patched up, but she was her father's daughter; and within four years of her own marriage Lisa cheated on her husband and walked out on him because she could not see the logic of staying with someone she no longer loved—

"We're all rational people here," Jordan said to his wife and children the day after he packed his suitcase and moved in with Sharon with no explanation other than "I'm leaving you." His wife and children were sitting at the kitchen table too shocked to speak. It was Saturday, and Jordan had come back to mow the lawn as he always did every second Saturday morning, and when he finished cutting the grass he walked into the house and took a cold beer out of the fridge and took two big swigs and then he took off his wedding band and put it on the kitchen table and said, "I don't love your mother anymore, and I can't see the logic of staying here—"

His wife and children were too traumatized to speak. He took one last swig of beer and left without saying another word; that's how his marriage ended. But Jordan Hansen had no idea what led to that callous moment of betrayal. That didn't begin to surface until one day a cocky student from Alberta pricked his conscience in his Grade Twelve English Literature classes with something he said that wormed its way into his soul and woke him up to his hypocritical life—

"*You think you're a Teacher Man like Frank McCourt, Mr. J; but you're not. You're so phony you think you're real,*" his cocky student responded when he was proven right in front of the whole class, to Jordan's absolute horror.

Jason Michaels was like no other student Jordan had ever taught. He didn't have a pretentious bone in his entire body, which gave him a natural gravitas that either attracted or repelled you; and it repelled Jordan from his first day in class.

It started with the class discussion of Frank McCourt's memoir *Angela's Ashes*. Jordan had assigned the class to write a book report, and when he handed them back Jason Michaels put up his hand and asked why the word "juxtaposed" was crossed out in red ink on his paper, and in the margin Jordan had written "NO SUCH WORD" in capital letters.

As if he had been pitted in a life-and-death joust with his student from their first encounter when Jason Michaels was transferred from another school in Calgary in the middle of the first term, Jordan trusted his own intellect enough to not even consider looking up the word in the dictionary, and his foolish pride became his undoing because Jason Michaels humiliated him in front of his whole class—

"Look it up and you'll see I'm right," Jason challenged.

"I don't have to look it up. Juxtaposed is not a word."

"You're wrong, teacher man," Jason replied.

"I'll look it up," volunteered Colleen Mackinnon, who thought Jason was the coolest boy in the whole school, and she went up to the shelf beside the blackboard at the front of the class and pulled out the Oxford English Dictionary and looked up the word "juxtaposition."

She found the word "juxtapose" and read the definition for the class to hear, with a big smirk on her pretty freckled face because she quickly saw that it favored the new student Jason Michaels. "Okay, this is what the dictionary says," she said, her eyes looking directly at Jason before reading: "Juxtapose, verb transitive. 1. place (things) side by side. 2. (followed by *to, with*) place (a thing) beside another; juxtaposition, noun; juxtapostional, adjective. *Jason's right, Mr. J!*"

Jason broke into laugher, and the whole class followed; and then Jason rubbed it in by saying that Mr. J was no Frank McCourt and called him a phony Teacher Man in front of all his students, and Jordan's humiliation was so devastating that it pierced his soul and shone a terrifying light into the darkness of his *shadow* self, and his ego collapsed in front of his students and changed his life forever.

He lost his self-respect that day, which had taken him his whole life to build, and he began his descent into the hell of his disingenuous life.

5. The Flip-flop

It was a classic male midlife crisis. Jordan never wanted to move to Winnipeg, Manitoba in the first place; but that was where his wife had to be for her hard-won career with the Royal Bank of Canada.

Maria was offered her first managerial position for the RBC in a new mall in Winnipeg and she could not say no, and Jordan, whom she had put through three years of university and one year of teacher's college, was not in a position to object; but he did insist on one condition: after five years they would return to southern Ontario, no matter what—

They moved from Oakville to Winnipeg with their children Mark and Lisa and settled into an apartment. Jordan began supply teaching, but he secured a fulltime position the following year at Regency High School where he was doing most of his supplying for the English teacher who ended up committing suicide to hasten the end of his cancer-ridden life, and the following year they bought their first house which they upgraded the following summer with Maria's brother Peter's help.

The five-year limit came and went before they knew it, but Jordan still longed to live in southern Ontario; and after fourteen years of Winnipeg's unbearable winters he put his foot down and told his wife they were moving back to Ontario.

His wife was taking another course for the RBC. She was forever taking courses to safeguard her career, which posed a low-threshold stress on their marriage; but her last course promoted her to a bigger bank and bumped her salary beyond her husband's reach, and though he tried not to let it show it ate away at his self-esteem and began to alter the dynamics of their relationship.

But it wasn't his wife's new promotion and bump in salary that bled Jordan's ego, it was the cumulative effect of little things that eroded his self-esteem, like having to do the grocery shopping and other household and family chores because Maria was always taking courses and catching up on her work on weekends; and then came the final humiliation of not being able to secure a teaching position when he put his foot down and demanded they return to southern Ontario.

Jordan was only offered one interview in the rural community of Lindsay after sending out thirty-nine resumes; and to push him over the edge, when he returned to Winnipeg from his interview his wife, who was in Banff for yet another course for her position at the larger branch that she was given, told her husband over the phone that she was not going to move to Lindsay or anywhere else unless the RBC secured her transfer; that's when Sharon saw her opportunity and propped up his wounded ego and cracked open the sacred matrimonial door for his unwitting betrayal.

Jordan dreamt of being in Ontario for his fortieth birthday, but when Sharon got her clutches into him his fate was sealed. The dream he had been nursing for fourteen years got shattered with thirty-eight rejections and his wife's refusal to relocate without a definite transfer, and his ego took such a terrible beating that he needed a shoulder to cry on; and the more Sharon Henderson listened to his mid-life woes, the more self-assured and secure Jordan felt.

"You understand me better than my wife does," he said to Sharon over coffee after school one day while Maria was still away in Banff, Alberta; and the following day Sharon invited Jordan to her condo for a cold beer and nice long talk just to clear his head. "One colleague to another," she said, with her toothy smile; and to sweeten the invitation his colleague added in her sincerest voice, "Friend to friend," and he could not say no to her because he was hurting so badly.

Sitting back on her living room sofa, Jordan talked and his colleague listened, and he drank another beer and talked some more and his colleague listened, and when his colleague handed him a third beer she sat beside him on the sofa and Jordan felt so comforted by his colleague that he found himself in her arms, and from that fateful moment on he continued to cheat on his wife; but Maria and the children did not suspect a thing. He told them he was golfing, and his family had no reason to suspect his lying and infidelity; but Jordan's personality began to change.

He was curt, less tolerant than usual, and much more demanding than he had ever been, and very attentive to his appearance. He was furtive and forever on the go, as if a foul wind was always blowing at his back; and he spent more time than usual in his den, talking on the phone with his colleague. But still Maria did not suspect a thing, not even when they made love, which was infrequent; and when Sharon knew she finally had him (she had exhausted herself massaging his ego), she gave him an ultimatum and he packed his suitcase and left his wife the following day.

Maria was shell-shocked, and her brother Peter took a leave from his uncle Frank's construction firm where he worked off and on for years and drove two thousand miles to console his younger sister; but still Maria had to see her family doctor for medication for her health and her career; and her children, who idolized their father who could do no wrong, could not believe he was capable of such a thing, and it ripped their heart apart and sunk them into despair.

Jordan took Mark and Lisa out for dinner two weeks after he moved into Sharon's condominium and tried to explain his decision, with all the calm objective reason that he was known and respected for; but as they listened to their father they did not recognize the man they thought they knew and loved.

"His face is even different," Mark said to his mother. "I can't explain it. It's his eyes, and the way he looks; he's just different. He's not the father I know."

"Yeah," Lisa said, with tears in her swollen eyes. "I don't recognize him either. It's like he's still my father but in a different body that looks like my father—"

Lisa broke down and cried inconsolably. Maria held her in her arms and cried with her. They didn't stop crying for hours. Mark went to his friend's house; but the next time Mark saw his father, he simply asked: "Why, Dad?"

"Because life happens, that's why," Jordan replied, impervious to his son's feelings. "It's a long story, Mark; and I don't expect you to understand until you get married and have children of your own. People grow apart. That's just the way life is. It happens to everybody. Your mother and I grew apart. It's not complicated. "

"Just like that? You broke up our family because you and Mom grew apart? Why couldn't you grow back together again? Did you even try? Mom said she never saw it coming. None of us saw it coming. Why didn't you talk to Mom? You just got up and walked out on us. What kind of man does that to his wife and family? No explanation. Nothing. You throw your ring on the table and walk out on us. What kind of man does that? That's cruel. I'm eighteen, Dad; I'm not a kid anymore. I understand some things. Why didn't you try to patch it up with Mom? Why?"

"It was too late. We grew apart, Mark. There was nothing left to patch up. It's not complicated. Why can't you see that?"

"It's not complicated for you because you always get what you want, but what about us? What do we get out of this? You broke up our family, Dad; and I don't understand why. It's not enough to say you and Mom grew apart. That's not a good enough reason. It's not, Dad. *It's not!*"

"That's life, kid; get over it," Jordan reacted—*the exact same words that his father said to him when his best friend was run over and killed by a drunk driver*—and Mark felt like he had just been kicked in the stomach by his own father.

That was the last time Mark spoke to his father; but after three long talks with his daughter she met the other woman and Lisa gave in and forgave her father and continued her relationship with him, and Sharon taught Lisa how to drive.

Maria could not forgive Jordan for his betrayal, but she moved on with her life and started dating again; and three years later married an electrician who owned his own business who strangely enough had also walked out on his wife and son and daughter the year he turned forty, and as hard as it was to believe—*"You've stepped into a parallel universe,"* Peter whispered into Maria's ear on the dance floor of their wedding reception, with a chuckle at the bizarre coincidence—his own son Derrick wanted nothing to do with him just as Jordan's son Mark wanted nothing to do with his father, but Derrick's sister Julie patched things up with her father just like Mark's sister Lisa. *"Life repeats itself,"* Peter said to his sister, with an ironic chuckle. *"But it doesn't matter what we do, sis; the gods will not be cheated."*

As much as Maria loved her favorite brother, Peter was too deep for her; but three years after Jordan walked out on his family and moved in with Sharon, Jordan's brazen student Jason Michaels delivered the critical blow that shocked him out of his complacency, and like the humbled lawyer Jean-Baptiste Clamence in Camus' tragic novel Jordan began his descent into the unforgiving hell of his undoing.

6. Tip of the Iceberg

As life goes, it didn't seem all that important; but Jordan's ego wouldn't let him forget, and day by day he festered over his foolish humiliation.

Something about Jason Michaels threatened Jordan's moral center, something he couldn't put his finger on but which he sensed was sacred and beyond his reach; that's why their energies clashed in his classroom. And it came to a head three weeks after his humiliation with what Jason said about a novel that Jordan had assigned before the Christmas break; Jason didn't like *The Fountainhead* by the atheist writer Ayn Rand, and he boldly told Mr. J—

"I don't agree with the novel's premise," Jason commented, sounding much older than his years. "Howard Roark is flawed. He has a hole in his soul. He's too much of an intellectual to be whole. Too much head and not enough heart. I think he's too selfish and self-serving to be a complete man."

The class waited for Mr. J's reply. He cleared his throat. "How else can you be your own man if you don't resist the social forces that keep you from realizing your own interests? Self-interest isn't a vice," Mr. J nervously countered his precocious student from Alberta. "Self-interest is an honorable virtue when viewed in the context of one's desires and aspirations. Personally, I embrace Rand's philosophy of rational self-interest. It's the only logical way to live your life."

"I see life differently," Jason Michaels replied, with the assurance of an old soul that was mistaken for uncanny wisdom. "You can't put life into a little box like Rand does with her philosophy. Life's too big to be framed by the mind, regardless how brilliant one may be. You have to have heart to be a whole person, Mr. J; and I think Rand's philosophy of rational self-interest smothers the human soul."

The class was mesmerized by Jason Michaels, who intimidated Jordan even more than his Nietzsche-loving father; but in a different way. He didn't know how far he could pursue it, but to save face phony Teacher Man had to give it his best shot—

"Perhaps; but only if you believe we have a soul, which Rand and I don't," Mr. J replied, and paused to take a breath. "This life is all we have, kid; and we have to make the most of it. That's why I put Ayn Rand on your reading list, so you can see what the real world is all about. Rand sees the world for what it is, a jungle; and you have to fight tooth and nail like Howard Roark for your individuality. Ego is all we have, and if you want your life to have any meaning you have to embrace who you are without prejudice. Does anyone else have an opinion?" asked Mr. J, hoping for a class discussion to take the pressure off himself.

Jordan's personal philosophy, which his favorite author had worked out with scintillating brilliance into a philosophy of rational self-interest that she called Objectivism, was conceived in a small farm in rural Saskatchewan near the potash mining community of Esterhazy with every farm chore that he was ordered to do by his hard-hearted father to earn his mortal keep.

"Nothing is free in this world," Eric Hansen told his children after slaving in the potash mine for years to save enough money to buy his farm, "not even your own life. You owe your life to your mother and me. That's a cold hard fact of nature, and you're going to earn the life we gave you or you can pack your things and leave—"

Eric Hansen had inverted the equation: his children owed him, not he the children. That was how he raised them; and each of his four children couldn't wait to get out into the world to live their own life. Jordan was the last to leave the family farm and Esterhazy and his native province of Saskatchewan.

The same day of his high school graduation Jordan packed his clothes into an old suitcase, kissed his mother goodbye and told his father, who spitefully refused to attend his graduation because he had to muck out the barn that Jordan refused to do on his graduation day, that he was leaving; and he hitchhiked to Ontario.

Jordan's second ride took him all the way from Esterhazy to Winnipeg, and from Winnipeg he got a lucky ride to Port Hope in southern Ontario and started working as a short order cook in the restaurant owned by the man who had picked him up in Winnipeg who was on his way home from visiting his ailing mother in Steinbeck; but Jordan didn't want to work in a kitchen for the rest of his life, and he went to Oakville with one of the waitress's boyfriend and applied for a job at Longo's food market and two weeks later was hired and met Maria Augustino one Saturday morning shopping for freshly baked Calabrese round bread and vegetables from the department that he was assigned to keep neat and freshly stocked.

They struck up a conversation over the broccoli-like vegetable called rapini, which Jordan had never seen before. "I guess you can cook them any number of ways," Maria responded to his inquiry; "but in our family we usually sauté them with olive oil and garlic and add a little salt and pepper, and we serve them as a side dish. My mother likes to add rapini to her olive oil and garlic pasta dish as well. It's not a vegetable Canadians are very familiar with."

"What does rapini taste like?" Jordan asked.

"Slightly bitter; but it's very good, and good for you. We love it in our family. We also eat dandelions prepared the same way, or in a salad," Maria offered, to Jordan's utter surprise. He had never heard of anyone eating dandelions before.

"You eat dandelions?" he asked, just to keep Maria talking.

"Not the flower," Maria said, laughing at the expression on Jordan's face. "We eat the green leaves. We love dandelion salads in our family. My mother goes out every spring to pick fresh dandelions in our yard and in the park down the street from our home; but the *mangiacakes* think we're crazy."

"*Mangia*—?"

Maria laughed. "A *mangiacake* is a Canadian who..."

That's how they met, and they talked every time Jordan saw Maria in the store, and then Jordan bit the bullet and asked her out on a date.

To his surprise—because Jordan never attracted girls in high school, what with his larger than average French mother's nose and unhandsome longish face that he inherited from his Norwegian father, which he made somewhat distinctive with a goatee when he started going to university after he married Maria, and glasses that he wore from the age of seven—she accepted; and on their third date they had sex in his old Beetle Volkswagen, which was the first time for them both, and Maria got pregnant and they had to get married to preserve the Augustino family honor.

That's how Jordan Hansen became the newest member of the proud Augustino family; but walking down the aisle of St. Andrew Roman Catholic Church in Oakville in a white dress was a real dilemma for Maria, the beautiful raven-haired princess of the Augustino family, so she called her brother Peter who was in San Francisco on another one of his trips to "Sanctuary" and pleaded for his advice.

There was a long pause on the phone. Peter cleared his throat, and said, "Maria, this may be the most difficult decision of your entire life; so please think carefully before you decide. If you wear white on your wedding day, you're going to build your marriage on a lie; and you will pay for it down the road..."

It took every ounce of courage that Maria had, but she wore a pale yellow gown that shocked her family and Italian community, but it also earned her the virtue to suffer whatever indignity life could throw at her, including the devastating blow of her husband's brutal betrayal eighteen years later.

Maria was Head Teller at one of the local branches of the RBC in Oakville, but her dream was to be manager of her own bank; so she took courses to upgrade herself, which was how she ended up in another branch as Loans Officer, and two years later

Assistant Manager; and beside his job at Longo's, Jordan sold vacuum cleaners door to door in the evenings and weekends until he decided to go back to school when a customer suggested that he get a teacher's certificate.

"We've got incredible job security no matter what the economy does, and one of the best pension plans in the world, not to mention every weekend and summers off," boasted the twenty-seven year old high school teacher who never bought a vacuum cleaner but whose smugness changed the course of Jordan's life.

Maria sacrificed to put Jordan through university, but it was worth it for her husband to obtain his teaching certificate; and when they moved to the windy city to her new position she finally realized her dream of having her own bank; but Maria still had a driving need to grow in the RBC while her husband was content to teach school all winter and golf all summer until he was ready to retire in Ontario, and he grew so complacent that he took his life for granted until one day that was no different from any other a student exposed him for the fraud that he had become.

Imagined or not, Jordan heard students laughing behind his back when he walked down the halls and in the cafeteria, and even when he wasn't in school he heard whispering and giggling in his mind, which only greased his descent into the hell of his guilty conscience; and day by day he became more conscious that his life was built upon the lie that he was master of his own fate; but he wasn't.

Jordan had a hole in his soul, and he began to see that his life, for all of the comfort and security that he had, *really* was contingent and absurd like the writers he loved and taught believed; and to ease the growing burden of his "curse of consciousness"—a phrase that Jason Michaels had brought to his attention when they were studying the works of Joseph Conrad, another one of Jordan's favorite writers—he drank to numb the gnawing pain of self-awareness.

"You're drinking too goddamn much, Jordan," Sharon began to harp. "You better cut back or you're going to end up just like Tobin!"

Twice divorced, Eric Tobin was their resident alcoholic, and Tobin wasn't the only alcoholic teacher in the school; just the most obvious with his extended beer belly and bulbous red nose. But Jordan didn't like being told how much he could drink, and he fought for his independence—

"I'll drink as much as I goddamn well please," he fired back one day, which became a daily ritual until he could stomach his life no longer and resigned his teaching position and left Sharon high and dry like he had done to his first wife and children, but for different reasons; and he packed his Toyota Corolla and drove to Georgian Bay, Ontario in search of a new life and self-redemption...

7. The Gnostic Way

When Jordan pulled into Elmer's yard two weeks later, he didn't know what to expect; so he played it safe and started mowing the lawn. Elmer opened the door and waved him into the house. Jordan shut the tractor down. "Morning, Elmer."

"Good morning. I've got a fresh pot on. Have coffee with me."

Jordan looked at him, wondering what game he was playing; but he quickly decided to find out. "Sure, why not?"

Elmer poured the Columbian blend that he ground himself into the same two mugs as before, Jordan's a deep forest green and Elmer's a clear sky blue, and set them on the table. Jordan asked if he could light a cigarette. "I prefer you didn't smoke in my presence. Smoking's a negative habit that pulls soul down to its lower animal nature, and my duty is to lift soul up to its divine nature."

Jordan grimaced. *"What?"*

"I could have said that smoking isn't good for your health, which it certainly isn't given all those carcinogens; but I wanted you to catch a glimpse of the spiritual side of life. That's what Jason wanted you to see."

"Jason? Jason who?" Jordan asked.

"Your English Lit student, Jason Michaels," Elmer answered.

Now Jordan was blown away. *"What the hell's going on here?"*

"Take a drink of coffee and calm down. I have something I want to share with you that will help you redeem yourself," Elmer calmly replied.

"Redeem myself? Look, I don't know who you are or what you're up to; but you're freaking me out. What's this all about, anyway? And how do you know Jason Michaels? Are you from Winnipeg?"

"No, I'm not from Winnipeg. I'm from God. And I'm here to help you step onto the path that will set you free from your private hell—"

Jordan jumped to his feet. "Look, if you're some kind of spiritual nut I don't want any part of this. *I don't believe in God!*"

"Belief's a mental thing, Jordan," Elmer replied, motioning with his hand for Jordan to calm down. "Buddhists don't believe in God either, but they're also seeking freedom from this hellhole we call life. You don't have to believe in God to free yourself from the cycle of life and death, but it helps. Sit down. Take a load off your feet. I'm not going to bite you. And I'm certainly not trying to convert you. I couldn't even if I wanted to, because life's a personal journey. I'm going to lay the facts of life out for you, that's all. You're ready to hear the truth, Jordan."

"What truth?" Jordan said, and nervously sat down.

"What do you think you're in this world for, anyway? Do you think your father was right? Do you honestly believe that this is all we have? That's the mind speaking, Jordan. The mind is the slayer of the real, and the disciple of truth must slay the slayer. Like I said, you've been called, and it's your turn at bat."

A thousand questions went through Jordan's mind. He looked at Elmer, afraid to stare too long; but once again he felt so much love pouring out of the strange man's eyes that his whole body began to tremble.

"Don't fret," he heard Elmer say. "That's just the Holy Current of God working its way through the negative patterns of your body. Nothing to worry about."

His body stopped trembling. "I have to go," Jordan said, and shot out the door like a bat out of hell. Elmer followed him out. Jordan jumped onto his tractor and continued mowing the lawn as quickly as he could so he could leave. Elmer watched him for a few minutes, and then went back into the house.

When he was done mowing and weed-eating, Jordan didn't know what to do. He wanted to get paid, but he was afraid of knocking on the door. Elmer came out with the money in his hand. "All done?"

"Yes," Jordan said.

"Good. See you in two weeks, then."

"I don't know," Jordan said, taking the money from Elmer's hand.

"You don't want to miss this train, Jordan. You paid your ticket for this ride a long time ago in another life; but that's neither here nor there. Come back when you've had time to think about what I said."

"Look, Elmer," Jordan said, swallowing hard; "I don't know what you're up to, but I don't understand anything you're saying. You're a very strange man."

"Of course I am, by your standards. But there are other ways to view the world, you know; and that's all I want you to see," Elmer said, and smiled.

"Why? What concern is that of yours?" Jordan asked.

"You've been called, that's why," Elmer replied.

"And what the hell's that supposed to mean?" Jordan said, angrily.

Elmer smiled again, his eyes bright with love. "God wants you back home, Jordan; that's what it means. There's no mystery to this thing called life. The problem with man is that he thinks too much. He should do less thinking and more right living. Do you really want to know who I am? I'll tell you. I'm a troubleshooter who goes from soul to soul to help them find their way out of the prison of their own misery. I heard your call, Jordan; and I'm here to help you. It's that simple."

"You heard my call?" Jordan said, more puzzled than spooked now.

"Yes. You called, and I came. Well, here I am. Take advantage of me. Ask me anything you want. What do you really want to know, Jordan?"

Elmer fell silent, waiting for Jordan to ask his question; but Jordan didn't know what to ask. He thought long and hard.

The silence was awkward; but finally he forced himself to look into Elmer's eyes, and said, "Why do I feel so empty?"

"You've lost connection with your inner self," Elmer replied, in a voice that was neither preachy nor sarcastic. "Once you step onto your path you will reconnect with your inner self and won't feel so empty anymore. It's a long way to your true self, Jordan; but you're here now, and I want to introduce you to yourself."

"Introduce me to myself?" Jordan said, with a quizzical frown.

"Didn't Jason Michaels tell you that to be a complete man you have to have heart? Well, the only way to get heart is to step onto your own path and live what the ancients call the Gnostic Way. The Gnostic Way is the way out of the emptiness of your life. You've found the Gnostic Way in me, Jordan. Don't blow it this time. You blew it three hundred years ago in Germany. Don't blow it again."

"*You're really freaking me out!*" Jordan exclaimed.

"Good. It's time someone shook your world. That's the problem with the world today; everyone is stuck in their mental self. Knowledge isn't the answer, Jordan; and neither is blind faith. *Knowing* is the answer. But to *know*, you have to *be*. And to *be*, you have to reconnect with your inner self and live the Gnostic Way; and this is what I'm here to help you do. *Capisce?*"

"Pardon?" Jordan said, taken aback by Elmer's Italian.

"You have no idea how fortunate you are, my young friend; but one day you will. The Gnostic Way is the way of the *knowing* heart. It's living your life honestly. You think you've been doing that all along, but you've been fooled by your own mind. Once again, Jordan; the mind is the slayer of the real, and the disciple of truth must slay the slayer. That's why Jason Michaels came to you. His job was to make you ready for the Gnostic Way. Get my receipt, will you. I have an appointment with another soul even more desperate than you; he's about to do himself in."

Jordan had it ready in his shirt pocket, but he was too dumbfounded to speak. He just stared at Elmer. Elmer snapped his fingers. *"Get with it, will you!"*

"What?" Jordan said, as if coming out of a trance.

"Where the hell's my receipt?"

"Right here," Jordan said.

"Good. I need it for those tax-grabbing bastards!" Elmer said, and snatched it out of Jordan's hand with that same contemptuous look on his wrinkled face.

Jordan was too startled to say anything. Elmer was doing it to him again, and he jumped into his truck and drove straight home and poured a stiff shot of rye and smoked and drank beer until he finally passed out.

8. The Golden Seed

It was like he was two people; a cranky old curmudgeon, and some kind of wise old magician, and Jordan didn't know what was happening to him. He had four more lawns to do, and all day he puzzled over what Elmer had told him. *"How does he know Jason? And what the hell does he mean that he's from God?"* His mind went back to Regency High School and Jason Michaels...

Out of curiosity, Jordan forced himself to read what was said to be the most translated book in the world next to the Christian Bible when Mrs. Brumby told the teachers in the staff room about it one Monday morning. *"The Alchemist,* by the Brazilian writer Paulo Coelho," she said, proudly holding the little book in her hand for everyone to see. "I was introduced to this book last week by one of my most gifted students. Jason Michaels. What a wonderful story. Jordan, you should read it."

"Why? It's not another one of your spiritual books, is it?"

"It is and it isn't. You have to read it to find out," Mrs. Brumby replied.

Jordan steered clear of those kinds of books, but because Jason Michaels had introduced her to *The Alchemist* it piqued his curiosity; so he stopped by Coles on his way home and bought a copy and read it after dinner.

"Crap," he said, as he read the story of the young Spanish shepherd boy's romantic quest for lost treasure in Egypt. *"Stuff and nonsense for the feeble mind,"* he vented, quoting one of his father's favorite expressions; and he wanted to throw the book away. But he had to find out what made Jason Michaels tick, so he read the story to the end; and in the staff room the next morning he held his copy for Mrs. Brumby to see, and said, "I read *The Alchemist* last night, Jane. Please tell me you don't buy into all this fairy tale nonsense of alchemy and lost treasure?"

"Don't be so cynical, Jordan. It's an allegory. It's not meant to be taken literally," replied the Social Studies teacher.

"Obviously. So what's all the fuss about, then?" Jordan asked.

"Why don't you ask Jason? He's in your Literature class, isn't he?"

"I will. But why don't you tell me why you like this book."

"It spoke to me here, Jordan," Mrs. Brumby said, touching her heart.

"Well it didn't speak to me here," Jordan said, touching his head.

"You know why that is, don't you?" Mrs. Brumby said, smiling wryly.

"No; but you're going to tell me, aren't you?" Jordan replied, sarcastically.

"Yes, I am. Because that," she said, touching her head, "has to be connected to this," she added, touching her heart. "*The Alchemist* is all about making this mind-heart connection. That's what makes it such a wonderful story."

Jordan regretted not asking Jason about *The Alchemist*, especially now that Elmer had mentioned his name. *"But how does he know Jason?"* he asked himself, plus a hundred other questions as he mowed his lawns; and by the time he finished his last yard he was so worked up that he drove straight to Elmer's house and knocked on his door and stepped back and waited anxiously for him to answer.

Elmer opened the door much sooner than he expected, like he was standing there waiting; but which Elmer? Jordan waited for him to say something, but Elmer just looked at him with a smile on his face and a ball cap without a logo on his head.

"I have to speak with you," Jordan said, coming right to the point.

"What took you so long?" Elmer said, and opened the door wide for Jordan to enter. "I've been waiting all day for you. Come in."

"You were waiting for me?" Jordan said, suddenly spooked again.

"Of course. Come in. I ground some fresh beans just for you. "

Jordan stepped inside and sat at the kitchen table. Elmer put on a fresh pot of an aromatic blend of roasted beans and sat down. "Well, you're here. Let's get it out into the open. Ask away. I'm all yours."

"Who are you?" Jordan quickly asked.

"Elmer Coventry," he replied.

"Where are you from?" Jordan asked.

"In this lifetime, from the USA. The state of Kentucky. I had one sister, but she died young. She was very talented and studied art in Paris. We were very close. She taught me how to soul travel and still comes to me in my dreams. I didn't know my mother, and I didn't care much for my stepmother. She didn't care for my spiritual interests. But my father did. He knew how to soul travel too, and we went everywhere together. I also had a stepbrother, but we didn't' get along. He was too much like my stepmother. I had a hard life growing up. I joined the navy to get a career, and when I got out I wrote for newspapers and stories for magazines. That's how I made my living. Then I was called to a higher purpose, and here I am today. Anything else you would like to know?"

"What do you mean, in this lifetime?" Jordan asked, as if everything else that Elmer said about himself didn't matter. "Have you lived before?"

"Soul lives many lifetimes, Jordan; and we just keep coming back until we get it right," Elmer replied, and took off his ball cap and hung it on his hat rack.

"Get what right?" Jordan asked.

"Life," Elmer said, sitting back down again.

Jordan was intrigued He thought his favorite writer had gotten it right, and he embraced her philosophy of rational self-interest; but look where it got him? "Just how does one get life right?" he asked, very nervous of the answer.

"The Gnostic Way," Elmer replied, and got up to get the coffee mugs.

"What does that mean?" Jordan asked, afraid of what he might hear.

"You know what Gnostic means, don't you?"

"Yes. It's from the Greek word gnosis. It means to know."

"Exactly. You have to know how to live life. That's the Gnostic Way," Elmer said, and reached into the cupboard for the blue and green mugs.

"That doesn't answer my question. How does one know how to live life?" Jordan asked, feeling a little more at ease by Elmer's agreeable manner.

"There is knowing, and there is *knowing*," Elmer said, emphasizing the second knowing. "Knowing with the mind and *knowing* with the heart are not the same thing. The Gnostic Way is the way of the *knowing* heart that has been awakened to soul's true purpose in life; that's the difference."

Suddenly Jordan thought of *The Alchemist* and jumped at the chance to find out how Elmer knew his puzzling student. "How do you know Jason Michaels?"

"We go back a long way, Jordan. He's working his end of the street, and I'm working mine," Elmer frankly answered, once more befuddling Jordan.

"I don't understand," Jordan said, suddenly feeling uneasy again.

"Jason Michaels is a Gnostic Master. He's here to harvest souls, as they used to say back in the day," Elmer said, and poured Jordan's coffee. The aroma was so strong that Jordan reached into his shirt pocket for his cigarettes, but he caught the look in Elmer's eye and put them back. Filling his own mug, Elmer added, "There are more things in heaven and earth than can be dreamt of in your philosophy, Jordan; but in time you will wake up to your true self and live the life you were meant to live. Is there anything else you would like to know?"

"Yes. Why do you pretend to be a cranky old man?"

"I never pretend, Jordan. I am a cranky old man."

"You're not a cranky old man now."

"I could be, if you want me to."

"I'd prefer you weren't. But I don't understand what you mean."

"I wasn't expecting to work on you this soon, but you cracked the door open when you decided to be your own man; so let's get started, shall we? Close your eyes and take a deep breath. There's nothing to fear...."

It happened again, Jordan was out of his body. Elmer took him by the arm and they sailed off to another world. Once again they were at a Temple of Golden Wisdom, this time on the Astral Plane, and again Jordan saw a large open book on a white lectern glowing in golden light, and a very striking man in a white robe and long blond hair and a radiance of love and wisdom walked up to them. "Welcome to the Golden Wisdom Temple of Askleposis, Jordan. Your journey has begun—"

"It began long ago," Jordan reacted, surprised by his own words.

Elmer and the man smiled. Then Elmer whispered into the man's ear and the guardian of the temple held out his fisted hand and opened it for Jordan to see. There was a golden seed in the palm of his hand, and he fisted his hand and pressed it firmly to Jordan's heart. Jordan felt a shock and jolted. The man took his hand away and Jordan swooned in blissful love and wanted to stay there forever—

"Would you like a refill?" Elmer asked.

"Pardon?" Jordan said, with a dazed look.

"Would you like some more coffee?" Elmer repeated.

"What happened?" Jordan asked.

"Not much. Just another golden seed planted."

"What golden seed?" Jordan said, not sure of where he was.

"You'll see in the fullness of time," Elmer said, his eyes twinkling. "Let's just hope the soil of your heart is a little more receptive this time," he added, with a little smirk on his face that didn't seem so wrinkled now. "And if not, you'll just keep coming back until you get it right—"

Jordan jumped to his feet. *"I have to go! I'll see you around—"*

"I'm sure you will. I'm always with you," Elmer said, and stood up and followed Jordan out the door. Jordan drove away more mystified than ever.

9. Fall from Grace

Jordan fell from grace the moment he betrayed his wife and children, and not until Jason Michaels called him a phony Teacher Man did he begin to see the hypocrisy of his own life; and he drank to dull the pain of his betrayal.

But as painful as it was, which took more and more beer to ease, Jordan justified his decision with his philosophy of rational self-interest; and he learned to live with the choice he made. *"I wasn't happy,"* he rationalized, *"so why should I suffer the rest of my life in a relationship that no longer made me happy? It was the logical thing to do,"* and he lit another cigarette and cracked open another beer.

That was the core of his philosophy, which was conceived on his father's farm at the tender age of twelve while slopping feed for the pigs and reasoned out with brilliant logic by Ayn Rand whom he discovered in grade eleven at Esterhazy High School, "Home of the Warriors" as his school was called. He didn't know how to express his feelings in the pig sty that day, but he knew one day his life would be his own; and he made a promise to himself that he would become a warrior and be his own man and no one would stand in the way of his happiness.

Like Ayn Rand, Jordan's happiness became his moral imperative, and before he left his father's farm he had crystallized in his philosophy of rational self-interest; and when he got home from his graduation he walked into the barn and said to his father, "I've paid my debt to you and mom for bringing me into this world, and I'm leaving now to live my own life," and when he walked down the gravel road from his house to the highway he never felt so lonely and free in his entire life...

Jordan cracked a beer and lit a cigarette when he got home from his last lawn of the day, and he opened the fridge and took out the rest of his roast beef and sliced an onion for a couple of beef and onion sandwiches. He missed Maria's cooking.

Sharon's cooking was boring after eighteen years of Maria's home-cooked Italian meals, but he never complained until he woke up to his life and Sharon began to annoy him in little ways that he once thought were endearing. One night Jordan woke up from a dream with Maria and his children (they were in Whistler skiing), and turning his lamp on he got the shock of his life to find a strange woman in his bed. He expected to see Maria, and all night long he went over in his mind how he ended up in bed with this other woman, and all the while he kept hearing Jason's voice, *"You're so phony you think you're real."*

Jordan got up and smoked and drank beer until Sharon got dressed for work. When she walked into the kitchen, she said, "This is too much, Jordan. You have to get a grip. I think you better get your ass to an AA meeting—"

Jordan sniggered in disgust, as much at himself as his wife; but this was the only way he could deal with the guilt of what he had done to Maria and his children, and day by day he resented Sharon a little more for stealing him away from them, and by the time he packed up and left he hated her and her toothy smile even more than he hated his own father who never once lied to him, and he vowed to redeem himself for what he had done to Maria and his children.

"You'll never make it out there on your own," Sharon taunted him whenever their arguments got nasty, which seemed to be every other day. "You're bought and paid for, Hansen. You're one of the we-people just like the rest of us civil servants!"

"Not for long," Jordan sniped, and took another swig of beer; and the following morning he got the shock of his life when he saw his other face in the mirror, and he began to plan his getaway. He had to prove to himself before he died that he could make it on his own, and he got all of his finances in order and resigned his position and moved to Hampton Beach in Georgian Bay to become his own man.

He traded in his Toyota Corolla for a pre-owned Dodge Ram four-wheel drive with a hitch and trailer and attachments for a snow plow, and he invested in a John Deer lawn tractor and push mower and weed eater and leaf blower and a twelve horsepower snow blower, and with less than forty thousand dollars he proudly started *Jordan's Lawn and Property Management Service* and put to use all of his mechanical and survival skills that he had learned on the farm from his father.

But to purchase the two-bedroom bungalow that he was leasing he had to appease his bank manager by assuring him that he was also supply teaching, which was a compromise he had to make for his new life in Georgian Bay, otherwise he could not secure the loan he needed for his mortgage; and though he could have taught more classes in the district, he tried to restrict himself to the Beach; but he enjoyed teaching now because he was his own man with his own business.

But still he felt empty, and he drank to kill the deadness of his depression. It crossed his mind to do himself in, but he never had the courage. *"I'm not a phony,"* he said to himself, *"and I don't have to prove anything to anyone. I don't owe anybody. I pay my bills. I vote. I'm responsible. I screwed up my life, but who hasn't?"* He cracked another beer and lit another cigarette and resigned himself to his situation. *"This is it, old man,"* he heard his father say. *"It's all you got, so make the most of it!"*

And then he met Elmer...

10. Elmer's Chicken Soup

Elmer threw Jordan's world into chaos. Twice he soul traveled with Elmer to a Temple of Golden Wisdom in the other worlds, and he had no explanation for what he experienced there, not to mention Elmer's split personality that challenged his psychology of human nature; but still, the love that he felt from Elmer made him feel so special that it gave him a new reason for living.

"You asked me why I think we're here," Jordan said to Elmer (he felt compelled to drop by on his way home from work one day, like he was being pulled by an invisible chord, and Elmer invited him in for a bowl of homemade chicken soup and pastrami sandwich), "and the only rational answer I can give you is that we're here because this is just the way life is. Nature evolved us into what we are, and when we die we die. That's all there is. That's what I believe. What do you believe?"

Elmer smiled at Jordan, like a father smiling at a child asking why the sky was blue. "As I said, that's the mind speaking," he said, and crumbled some crackers into the hot broth of his chicken soup that hit Jordan's nostrils the moment he stepped through the door because it reminded him of Maria's chicken soup that she made whenever they had a cold or the flu. "The mind is nature's computer, recording and computing the life process," Elmer continued, looking at Jordan who was spooning soup into his mouth like he had forgotten what good homemade chicken soup tasted like. "But is the mind *sui generis*?" Elmer asked, rhetorically. "Yes and no. Man's mind has evolved with the life process, and it is perforce *sui generis*; but it is not the prime mover. Love is the prime mover. Love is the essential energy of the universe, and the creator of all life. Love makes the world go round, as the saying goes. It's ironic, but man has all the answers that he needs right here," Elmer said, tapping his chest. "Of course, the heart is a metaphor for our divine nature. This is why the Gnostic Way is called the way of the *knowing* heart. *Capisce*, Jordan?"

Maria's brother Peter, who was the black sheep of the Augustino family and with whom Maria was so close that it made Jordan jealous whenever he came to visit, used the word *capisce* to punctuate his point, and it always irritated Jordan because it sounded so cocky and self-assured. He took a bite of his pastrami sandwich to give him time to think. He couldn't dismiss Elmer as a spiritual nut, because he didn't really strike him that way; he was just strange, and as much as he wanted to challenge Elmer, he didn't know how. But he couldn't accept what he said on faith alone either. That's why his father hated religion, especially Christianity.

"What proof do you have?" he finally said, remembering Bertrand Russell's book *Why I Am Not a Christian* that his father gave him for his twelfth birthday.

"Proof? For what?" Elmer asked.

"That God exists," Jordan said.

"You can't prove the existence of God. No one can. You can only experience God. You have to initiate yourself into the mysteries of life, Jordan. I can help you make the connection, but you have to come to your own realization of God's existence. Now let's get back to the issue of natural evolution, because this is where the atom of God enters into life to begin its climb up the ladder of evolution."

"What do you mean by atom of God?" Jordan asked, and spooned the last of his chicken soup. Elmer ladled some more hot broth into Jordan's bowl, this time adding some pieces of chicken meat to give it more substance.

"Thank you," Jordan said. "This is really good."

"Chicken soup for the soul," Elmer said, with an ironic smile that Jordan failed to appreciate. "Now, where were we?"

"I was asking you about the atom of God," Jordan said.

"Oh, yes. An atom of God is the seed of a new soul, a tiny spark of divine consciousness that exists in every person. Every living thing began as an atom of God in the Ocean of Love and Mercy. This is a metaphorical name for the Body of God, of course; and God sends its atoms into these lower worlds to evolve into spiritually self-realized, God-conscious souls. But nature can only evolve an atom of God to the state of reflective self-consciousness, not spiritual self-realization consciousness; that comes later, when man takes evolution into his own hands. Quite simply, God needs life to become more God. This is the essential purpose of life. But as I said, nature can only evolve the atom of God until it gives birth to a new 'I' of God, and no further. To realize his divine nature man must complete what nature cannot finish by taking evolution into his own hands. This is where the Wayshower comes into the picture. This was the higher purpose that I was called to, and my reason for offering you my chicken soup. Now you know the back story to the old saying, 'when the student is ready, the teacher appears.' Is that clear enough for you now?"

Jordan's legs were trembling. He was in awe. He felt privileged, like he had been chosen for a higher purpose; and love filled his heart. Then in a voice that sounded like his grade eight teacher Mr. Sparks when he calmed his fear of going into high school, Elmer spoke again, "The first thing you have to do is drop your fear of the unknown. Only then can you proceed."

"Where to?" Jordan asked, in his young boy's voice.

"To your true self," Elmer said, with love pouring out of his eyes.

"What do you mean, my true self? Isn't this who I am?" Jordan said, taping his chest with his spoon-free hand and his legs still trembling.

"That is the body you use to realize your divine nature. Science and religion have it backwards, Jordan. Science says this is all there is, and religion tells us that man has an immortal soul; but the truth is that soul evolves through the body, and it continues to evolve with every new life until it breaks the cycle of life and death."

"I don't believe we have a soul," Jordan said.

"So what? Just because you don't believe you have a soul doesn't exempt you from karma and reincarnation. You have no choice. No one does. Soul is the ground of all being and the essence of who we are, and waking up to our divine nature is what the journey through life is all about. But as I said, man needs help to find the way to his true self. This is where I come in. You called, and I'm here."

"I don't remember calling you," Jordan said.

Elmer smiled. "Like most people, you made it impossible to free yourself from the prison of your own nature, and your soul cried for help. I had to come, Jordan. It's my duty as the Wayshower to assist every soul in need of help. *Capisce* now?"

Again with that word. "No, I don't understand," Jordan said, suddenly aware of where he was. "This is too much. Do you mind if I come back another time?"

"No, I don't mind. But remember, you don't have to talk to me in person to get the answers you're looking for. Just think of me, and I'll be there for you."

Jordan stared in bewilderment; and as he drove home he could still taste Elmer's incredible chicken soup, and his legs still trembled.

11. Elmer's House

Jordan wasn't aware of it, but when he dropped in to ask Elmer a few questions he had begun the journey to his true self; and as much as his mind resisted the implications, he couldn't stop thinking of the effect that Elmer was having upon his life; that's why he couldn't stop his legs from trembling.

He had never met anyone like Elmer. He looked like an ordinary old man, but he was far from ordinary. He was some kind of mystic, and Jordan didn't know what to make of him. He had grown up not believing in God, despite his mother's strong Catholic faith, which his father ridiculed to undermine his wife's authority over their children, so he avoided reading books on religion and spiritual teachings because his father had convinced him they were a waste of time; but Elmer had opened the door to the spiritual side of life, and this threw Jordan's world into confusion.

When he went to sleep that night, after five beer and a shot of rye, he had a strange dream. He was in his mother's womb, but he wasn't in his body yet; he was outside his mother's body while experiencing his body forming in his mother's womb. He was in and out of his own fetal body, like he was split in two. When he woke up he didn't know what to make of his dream, and he tried to dismiss it from his mind; but all day long he pondered what it meant and thought of asking Elmer.

He had a busy day trying to catch up on his lawns, so he had no time to drop over; but on his way to work the following day he drove by Elmer's house and got the shock of his life; *Elmer's house was gone and there was a different house on the lot!*

Jordan checked the house number, and it was the right one; but he might have taken the wrong street, so he drove back to the end of the street and read the sign: *Bayfield Boulevard.* It was the right street, so he drove back to Elmer's house and stared at the red brick split-level that was supposed to be a bungalow with gray vinyl siding, and a chill ran up his spine. He lit a cigarette to steady his nerves.

As he smoked his cigarette he studied the neighbor's house to the left and the neighbor's house to the right, and they were the same houses that he remembered, and then he wondered if Elmer Coventry lived there at all; but he didn't have the courage to knock on the door and find out, so he sat in his truck and lit another cigarette hoping that everything would return to normal.

He heard a tap on his window, and it startled him. It was a silver-haired gentleman who had read the sign on Jordan's truck and wanted to know what he charged for looking after his house when he went to Florida for the winter and keeping his driveway clean of snow. Jordan gave him his rates and wrote them down on his business card and then asked if he knew the man who lived in the house where Elmer Coventry's house was supposed to be.

"I don't know the man personally, but I've seen him when I go for my walks," said the silver-haired gentleman. "He's retired. I believe they're snowbirds."

"They?" Jordan asked.

"Him and his wife."

"Oh," Jordan said.

"Are you doing their lawn?"

"I think I got the wrong address," Jordan said.

"Alright, then. I've got your card. I'll call and let you know if we decide to go to Florida this winter."

"Just leave a message if I'm not home."

"Okay, thank you. Have a nice day," said the man, and turned to walk away.

"You too," Jordan said, and lit another cigarette. He didn't know what to do, so he just sat and smoked. All kinds of strange thoughts ran through his mind, but he could not think of a logical explanation for what was happening to him. *"Maybe it's my drinking, and I'm having some kind of alcohol-induced hallucination?"*

An elderly couple came out of the red brick split-level and got into their car, which was a different color and model than Elmer's, and Jordan stared as they drove out of the yard and down the street. He got a good look at the driver, and it wasn't Elmer Coventry; so he started his truck and drove away.

He couldn't see a doctor. He knew what he would say. But he also knew that what was happening to him was beyond his comprehension. Just to make sure he wasn't hallucinating, he drove by Elmer's house every day and the same red brick split-level was still there; and when Thursday came, the day that he was supposed to mow Elmer's lawn, he didn't know what to do, and he drove down Elmer's street slowly, like he was stalking a ghost in the dead of night, and there it was—

Elmer was standing in his yard waiting, wearing a little Greek fisherman's cap with a big grin on his face. "Good morning Jordan! How are you this fine morning?" he hollered, and walked up to Jordan and extended his hand for him to shake.

Jordan's face was white. He stammered, "You're here?"

"Where else would I be?" Elmer said, taking hold of Jordan's hand.

Jordan shook Elmer's hand but didn't know what to say, and he took out his cigarettes; but he caught the look in Elmer's eyes and put his package back into his pocket. "I don't know what's happening to me," he said, trembling like a leaf. "I came by here every day this week, but—"

"My house wasn't here," Elmer said, completing Jordan's sentence. "Don't worry about it, Jordan. Everything's back to normal. We can talk about this after you do the lawn. I'll go in and put on a nice fresh pot of coffee."

Jordan couldn't believe his ears. He needed a drink. "Look, I can't do your yard today. Do you mind if I come back Monday morning?"

"How about tomorrow?" Elmer asked.

"No. I'm booked all day tomorrow."

"Monday it is, then. Have a good day, Jordan," Elmer said, and went back into his house, the bungalow with vinyl siding. Jordan lit a cigarette to calm his nerves before driving away, completely forgetting to ask Elmer about the dream that was so important to him before his experience with Elmer's phantom house.

12. The Conversation

Jordan was in a quandary. He had no one to share his experience with, other than Elmer whom he believed was responsible for what was happening to him, and he didn't know what to do. He tried to put it out of his mind, but no amount of alcohol could make him forget what he had experienced; so he decided to face it head on, like his father had brought him up to do—

"No one's going to solve the problem for you," said Eric Hansen to his three sons and daughter, like a ritual mantra. "Whatever's bothering you, face it. In the end, you have no one but yourself; so work it out."

Jordan's father was a hard man, but he was a realist. Just then, Jordan thought of something that Elmer said when he invited him in for chicken soup and pastrami sandwich, "Just think of me and I'll be there for you," so he cracked another beer and said out loud, "I'm thinking of you now. What are you doing to me, Elmer?"

"What do you expect? Tilling the soil for the golden seed, of course."

Jordan jumped to his feet and frantically looked around, but there was no one there. He looked and looked, but there was no one. He checked to see if the TV was on, but it wasn't; and neither was his radio on the counter. *"What's going on?*

"You asked me a question, and I answered," Elmer's voice replied.

Again, Jordan started in fear. "I'm losing it," he said, and took a swig of beer. He waited. Nothing happened, and as he pulled on his beer again he thought of something and lit a cigarette. He expected Elmer to say something, but the room was so silent it sent a chill up his spine; and he puffed away until there was nothing left to puff on, and he finished his beer in awkward silence. But the silence got to him, and he spit out, *"Why me?"*

"Because you're ready," Elmer's voice replied.

"READY FOR WHAT?" he shouted, in desperate anger.

"To play the endgame," Elmer's voice replied.

"I DON'T WANT TO PLAY ANY GODDAMN ENDGAME WITH YOU!"

"It's not me you're going to play with," Elmer's voice responded.

"WHO THEN?"

"God."

"I DON'T BELIEVE IN GOD!"

"God believes in you. That's why I'm here."

"Is that you, Elmer?" Jordan asked, feeling rather stupid.

"Yes," Elmer said.

"Why are you doing this to me?"

"Because you're ready."

"I'M NOT READY FOR THIS!" Jordan shouted again in anger.

"Get a hold of yourself, Jordan. The neighbors might hear you."

"THIS IS TOO MUCH," he hollered, and jumped to his feet and ran into his garage and paced back and forth to calm down. And then he took out a warm beer from the twenty-four pack that he had on a pile of four full cases and took a long hard pull, and then another and killed it. He heard his father's voice in his mind, not literally: *"No one's going to solve the problem for you."*

He put his empty bottle into the case and went into the house and sat down in the living room where he had heard Elmer's voice. "Okay, I'm back. What's this endgame you want me to play? What do I have to do?"

"Let go of your fear," Elmer's voice replied.

"I don't give a damn any more. What do you want me to do?"

"Be yourself, Jordan; just be yourself," replied the discarnate voice.

"Be myself? What the hell is that supposed to mean?"

"Who were you when you were in your mother's womb?"

The question startled Jordan. "In my dream?"

"Yes. Who were you in your mother's womb?"

"I was me," Jordan replied, now more curious than afraid.

"And who were you when you were out of your mother's womb?"

Jordan thought for a moment, and replied, "I was me."

"And were you not the same person?" Elmer asked.

"Yes. No. I don't know. Was I?" Jordan stammered, all confused.

"When you taught the grade nine class on Friday, who were you?"

"I was me," Jordan said, automatically.

"And when you did Crawford's lawn Saturday, who were you?"

"I was me," said Jordan.

"And when you played golf with Derrick on Sunday, who were you?"

"I was me. Who else?"

"Yes, you were Jordan Hansen," said Elmer's discarnate voice. "You put on your teacher personality on Friday, your lawn maintenance personality on Saturday, and your golfer's personality on Sunday. You were the same person with three similar but separate personalities. Soul has many personalities, Jordan; but they're just personalities like the different clothes we wear for different occasions. The real you is soul, the individuated consciousness of all your personalities, past, present, and future; and the endgame is the final game of life that will liberate you from all your personalities that keep you bound to the cycle of life and death."

Jordan listened to Elmer's voice like he was listening to the TV without a picture. He caught himself listening to the voice and broke into hysterical laughter. *"I've really lost it this time,"* he said, and then froze in horror. *"Well?"* he challenged a few moments later, totally devoid of fear like a soldier no longer afraid to die.

Elmer didn't speak. When Jordan butted his cigarette, he challenged Elmer again, "I'm not smoking now. What do you have to say for yourself?"

"I think you should get some rest. Good night, Jordan."

Jordan didn't reply. He stared into empty space until he could sit up no longer and slumped over on the couch and fell into a deep sleep.

13. The Golden Seed of Gnosis

Was Elmer God? The thought was too much for Jordan, and he dismissed it from his mind. His mother believed in God and went to church every Sunday with her friend and neighbor Margaret, and as much as he loved his mother he was a nonbeliever like his father. He didn't want to be like him, and his greatest fear was that he would one day become like his father; but after many years away from the farm he had to admit that his father made a lot of sense about the world.

"If I can't see, hear, touch, smell, and taste it, it's not real. It's all up here, and what's up here changes like the prairie wind," his father used to say in that Zarathustrian way of his. "God is not dead. He was never alive, so how can he be dead? People need God because the alternative would crush them; but when you learn to live without God you see life for what it is, and then you grin and bear it."

That's how Jordan grew to savor the little pleasures of life. They gave his life the meaning that cushioned him from the world of suffering that Jesus promised to save his mother from with his death upon the cross. Like his father, the little pleasures of life were salvation enough for him. Of course, he knew that pleasure was fleeting, and that life was meaningless and absurd; but his father solved that for him with another one of his many sayings. *"Plan for tomorrow, but live your life today."*

Jordan built his life on this piece of paternal wisdom; and when he divorced Maria he invested his share of their almost mortgage-free home wisely planning for tomorrow, which turned out be his new life in Georgian Bay, Ontario. But now his world of sound reason and careful investments had come into contact with another world that he could not fathom, and he didn't know if he was going crazy.

The morning after his conversation with Elmer's voice, he showered and shaved and put on fresh clothes and fried half a package of bacon and three eggs and toasted four slices of bread and put on a fresh pot of coffee to start his day, and as he wiped up the last of the egg yolk and bacon fat with his toast he thought of the little prairie classic *Who Has Seen the Wind*, by W. O. Mitchell, a coming of age novel of a prairie boy called Brian that Jordan had taught for years to his grade ten students, and he comforted himself in the knowledge that he was not alone in his belief because none of his favorite writers believed in God either.

Jordan studied *Who Has Seen the Wind* in grade ten at Esterhazy High, and he identified with young Brian growing up. *"Everything that lives must die,"* Eric Hansen told his boys whenever they slaughtered another pig; and Jordan thought of his father's saying every time he had to kill a chicken for their family meal. And when he went to his first funeral and saw his first dead person, a neighbor who was killed working on his car when the old jack slipped and crushed him to death, lying in his coffin all pale looking like he was asleep, his father said to him, "Take one last look, old man; everything that lives must die."

Eric Hansen overheard his wife telling Jordan that Mr. Sodergren was in heaven now, and he scoffed at the idea. "That's a pipe dream, old man. There is no heaven; and there's no hell either, unless you want to call this life hell. Hank's gone to his grave for the worms to eat. That's where we all end up some day; including you, old man." His father called him old man for reasons he never understood, and as he reflected on his childhood he took one last drag on his after-breakfast cigarette and said, "God's not in the wind either. What do you think of that, old man?"

He was sober now, and he didn't expect Elmer to respond; but he got the shock of his life when Elmer shouted, "GOD IS!"

Jordan froze. He couldn't move. He just sat in his chair and stared into the empty kitchen. He was too scared to start another conversation with Elmer. He didn't want to contribute to his own insanity.

All morning he convinced himself that his conversation with Elmer was some kind of hallucination triggered by his drinking, but after his hardy breakfast he was as sober as could be, and he wasn't crazy; but Elmer spoke again, and he panicked.

"I'm not drunk," he said to himself. "I'm sober. I don't believe in God; I don't believe in life after death; and I don't believe in heaven and hell. God doesn't exist in the wind or anywhere else. "GOD ISN'T!" he shouted, unable to control himself.

"Have it your way, then," Elmer replied. "But you know you can't put it off, don't you? You can go on fooling yourself as long as you want, old man; but one day the pressure will be so great that you will crawl on your hands and knees to God looking for a way out of your misery. That's just the way it is, old man. It's your choice. I'm here now, and I'll be here when you come to your senses."

Jordan was too shocked to speak. He lit another cigarette. He took two puffs and waited for Elmer to say something more, but he didn't.

"I don't want to leave this life," Jordan finally said, unable to contain himself. "I like life, and I want to live as long as I can."

Elmer waited for Jordan to put out his cigarette. "Everything that lives must die, Jordan. Didn't your father tell you that?"

"Yes, but I don't want to die for a long time yet."

"Are you afraid of dying?"

"Isn't everybody?"

"No. Just those souls trapped by their own ego. You see, old man; life is all about overcoming death, not succumbing to it. This is the point of the endgame. It will teach you how to overcome death."

"You can't overcome death. No one can. And there's nothing after death. Just a big hole in the ground," Jordan replied, with a gnawing sense of doubt.

"Jordan, where's my body?" Elmer asked, with a smile in his voice.

"Pardon?" Jordan said, puzzled by Elmer's question.

"Where's my body? Is it in a hole in the ground somewhere? No. My body is at home reading today's paper; but I'm here too. You can't see me, but I'm still here with you. And I'm here to till the crusty soil of your stubborn mind. That's what all of this mystical stuff is about."

"Why?" Jordan asked, unable to resist himself any longer.

"So the golden seed can take root in your heart."

"I don't understand. What golden seed?"

"The golden seed of Gnosis that you received from the Master at the Temple of Golden Wisdom. For the golden seed to take root in man's heart, the soil of his mind must be receptive. Your mind has been hardened by your ego, old man. But regardless how hard the soil of man's mind may be, soul never stops growing; and when soul is ready to take evolution into its own hands and begin the final stage of its journey home to God, it calls to God for help and the golden seed is planted. That's why I'm here, to introduce you to the Gnostic Way. *Capisce* now?"

That word annoyed Jordan. "No, I don't *capisce*!"

"Let me see if I can help you to understand, then," Elmer said, in a voice that sounded very familiar. "Sit back and listen, because I'm going to give it to you straight like your old man used to do whenever he lost his patience with you. Every person has two selves, one lower and one higher; and along with his two selves, man has two destinies: one karmic and one spiritual. Your lower self is responsible for your karmic destiny, and your higher self is pre-ordained. But your higher self can only grow through your lower self, and this is the mystery that no one seems able to resolve. Unfortunately your higher self can only grow so much through your lower self, and no more; so when one is ready to take evolution into their own hands and realize their spiritual destiny, they are given the golden seed of Gnosis to help the two selves become one; and you have been given the golden seed because you have been called to a higher purpose. Do you understand now?"

Jordan was glad that Elmer didn't punctuate his point with *capisce*, because it had the annoying effect of making him feel stupid; but still, he didn't understand. "What do you mean by lower and higher self? We only have one self, don't we?"

"Yes and no. Every person is a spark of divine consciousness. This is the seed of your higher self that grows as it evolves through its lower self; but as I said, man can only grow so much through the natural process of karmic evolution. For the spark of God to realize its divine nature, man has to take evolution into his own hands; but to do this man needs help. Like it or not, old man; you need me."

Jordan forgot that he was talking to a disembodied person, and he was about to respond when he realized that he was alone. "Why don't you show yourself, Elmer?" he said instead. *"Come on, show yourself!"*

"That would defeat my purpose."

"What purpose?"

"To till the soil of your mind. It's much easier to shock your mind out of its complacency if I don't appear to you."

"Am I going crazy?"

"No."

"I'm not losing my mind?"

"Yes, you are; insomuch that you're having a shift in consciousness from the mental to spiritual side of life. Your mind is just a little shocked, that's all."

"That's all?" Jordan exclaimed, and reached for his cigarettes.

"If you light it, I'm gone," Elmer said.

"I need a smoke," Jordan said, and flicked his lighter; but before he put the lighter to his cigarette he heard Elmer say, "One day you will have to decide which is more important; the pleasures of your little ego, or freedom from the despair of your empty lonely life. Have a nice day, Jordan—"

Jordan smoked his cigarette and waited for Elmer to return, but Elmer didn't; and all day long Jordan tried to speak with Elmer, but he got no response, and Jordan felt really stupid for letting his ego get the best of him.

14. Memories of his Father

For days, Jordan thought about what Elmer said about the lower and higher self and playing the endgame; but he didn't know what to do about it. He didn't know if any of it was real, and it threw him into a tizzy.

"Work it out on your own," his father used to say; which was a terrifying thing to hear when he was so young but fundamentally sound advice because it taught Eric Hansen's children to take the initiative. *"But how in the hell do I solve something I don't understand?"* Jordan said to himself, in utter frustration.

For some reason which he could not fathom, other than that he was called to a higher purpose, he had been introduced to another reality that played havoc with his mind; and he just didn't know how to deal with it. He chose not to go to Elmer's house until the day he mowed his lawn, but when he pulled into Elmer's yard he got the surprise of his life—

"Go away! I don't want you cutting my lawn today!" Elmer shouted when Jordan stepped out of his truck. Elmer was standing behind his half-opened door. *"Go on, get out of here! I don't need that noise today!"*

Jordan was certainly not expecting the cranky old man, not after their last two conversations, so he was momentarily shocked; but he quickly steeled himself and got his bearings. He was used to mood swings from his father, who one minute could be all smiles and reason and the next all temper and meanness, so he said, "I've got you scheduled for today, Elmer. I have to do your lawn this morning."

"Well if you have to you have to. Just make it quick. I've got another one of those goddamn headaches. I slept like shit last night!"

That kind of reality Jordan understood, and he smiled to himself as he mowed Elmer's lawn; but what happened to the other Elmer?

Jordan hadn't thought of his father for a long time, but Elmer's sudden change of mood reminded him so much of his father that memories came flooding in so fast he had to light a cigarette to settle down. *"Is he just playing at being cranky?"*

His father didn't play the bad tempered role; he was bad tempered and mean when his mood changed, and the whole family knew to stay out of his way. But Elmer—well, he didn't know what to make of him.

When he finished trimming the lawn he put his equipment away and knocked on Elmer's door. Elmer shouted, "I got no money today! My old age security didn't come in! Come back next week!"

"I want to talk to you!" Jordan shouted back.

"Get lost! I'm not in the mood for talking!"

"Don't play with me, Elmer!"

Elmer yanked the door open. "What did you say to me?"

"I said don't play with me."

"You think this is a game?"

"Yes, I do."

"Did your father play games with you?"

Taken by surprise, Jordan stepped back. "No, he didn't. My father never played games with us. He was all business."

"So am I. Now get lost. I've got a headache!"

Elmer slammed the door in Jordan's face and he had no choice but to leave; but he couldn't get Elmer out of his mind. Elmer was the cranky old man again, but the question that Elmer asked about his father came from the other Elmer, and Jordan couldn't make heads or tails of Elmer's behavior. *"What the hell's going on?"*

On his way home for lunch the next day, Jordan knocked on Elmer's door. Elmer answered. Jordan studied his eyes. If they twinkled, he knew he would be safe; and if they looked cold and suspicious, he had to watch himself. "Here's your money. Now get lost!" Elmer said, thrusting the money into Jordan's hands and shutting the door in his face again. Jordan went to his truck and wrote a receipt and knocked on Elmer's door and shouted, "I've got your receipt!"

"Stick it in the crack of the door!" Elmer shouted, not giving Jordan a chance to talk. Jordan knocked again. "I have to talk with you, Elmer!"

"Get lost! You're giving me a headache!"

"I have to talk with you!"

Elmer swung the door open and waved a knife in Jordan's face. "What the hell do I have to do to get through to you? *Get lost, I said!*"

Instinctively Jordan jumped back like he always did whenever his father raised his hand to strike him. "Alright," he said, and walked away; and when he got back into his truck he stroked Elmer off his list and said to himself, *"To hell with him. I don't need this shit!"*

15. Just Another Dream

There, now he didn't have to worry. Elmer was no longer in his life, and he didn't expect any more weird experiences, and for three days nothing happened; but then he had a dream that put the fear of God into him.

Jordan was driving his truck with his trailer and lawn tractor. He was on the 400 highway on his way to Carlton to have work done on his John Deer when his truck started sputtering and jerking and before he knew it a transport that was following couldn't slow down enough to stop crashing into the rear of his trailer and flipped it and threw his truck out of control and it rolled and crashed into the guard rails and kept sliding until it came to rest in a pile of smashed metal.

Jordan was killed, but he left his body and watched the whole scene from a vantage point outside his body. He was so startled by the experience that he didn't realize he was dead until he saw the paramedics pull his mangled body out of his truck and put it into a body bag and carry it away.

He didn't know what to do, or where to go. He walked up to an OPP officer and spoke to him, but the officer didn't hear him. He tapped him on the shoulder, but his hand went right through the officer's body and sent a chill up his spine. It was just like the movie *Ghost* with Patrick Swayze that he and Sharon had seen in the theatre in Winnipeg—*he was a ghost too!*

No sooner did he realize that he was a disembodied spirit and he was swooshed to another realm and was standing in front of a movie-like screen where he watched his whole life lived out from his birth to his accidental death, and he was so shocked at how selfish he had been throughout his life, especially with Maria and his children with all the time he squandered golfing, that he was overcome by an overwhelming sense of remorse and guilt.

He woke up drenched. He lit a cigarette and tried not to think about his dream, but he couldn't help himself. He had died but was still alive in another body. That wasn't supposed to happen. He went into the kitchen and cracked a beer and took a big swig. He drank his beer with another cigarette and tried to calm his nerves. *"It was just a dream."* But the dream was too real to be dismissed so casually, and he cracked another beer to calm his nerves.

He couldn't go back to sleep, so he put coffee on and sat at his kitchen table drinking coffee and smoking until it was time to go to Hampton High to teach for the day; so he showered and shaved and got dressed and lit another cigarette and drove to work very mindful of the road.

He was filling in for an English teacher who had to fly to Vancouver for her twin brother's funeral and would be off till Tuesday, and one of his students asked him if he had ever read Albert Camus.

"The French philosopher?" Jordan asked, not to give himself away.

"Yes. Have you read *The Outsider*?"

"A long time ago. Why, do you like Camus?"

The student nodded his head. "Yeah. I found *The Outsider* in my father's library and couldn't put it down. My father loves Camus, and we talk about his philosophy all the time. He sure makes you think, doesn't he?"

"I'm surprised he's still read today," Jordan said. "So, what does Camus make you think about?" he asked, curious about the boy's fascination.

"Do you think life is meaningless and absurd? Camus does," said the student. "My father thinks so too. What do you think, Mr. Hansen?"

"Let's ask the class what they think. Anyone?"

"What do you mean by absurd?" one girl asked.

"Camus says that life doesn't have meaning except the meaning that we give it. That makes life absurd," replied the Camus student.

"That's stupid," the girl said. "Of course life has meaning. Everything we do has meaning, doesn't it?"

"That's not what Camus thinks. You should read *The Outsider*. You'll get a whole new picture on life if you do. I sure did."

"Anyone else have an opinion?" Jordan asked, with an ironic smile.

"What about you, Mr. Hansen?" the Camus student asked. "Do you think life is absurd; or do you think it has intrinsic meaning?"

"I'm inclined to favor Camus. I think life is what we make of it," he answered, but his voice wasn't quite convincing.

"Do you think this life is all we have?" the Camus student asked.

A sudden chill shot through Jordan's spine as his death flashed across his mind. "What do the rest of you think? Do you believe in life after death? Let's have a show of hands for those who do," he said, curious to know how his students felt.

Everyone raised their hands except for the Camus student and another girl, and Jordan asked why they didn't think there was life after death.

The Camus student said, "I just don't. I think this life is all we have and we have to make the most of it." And the girl, whose father was a doctor, said, "I believe in natural evolution. I don't believe there is a Creator who made us. Nature made us, and when we die we go back to nature. Science tells us that energy can't be created or destroyed, so we don't really die; but the energy that made us goes back to nature and becomes something else. So we may become a fish or whatever; but that's not us. We die, but our life force goes back to nature. That's what I believe, anyway."

Jordan didn't want to open that door with his students, so he said: "Either way, we still have to make the most of life; don't we? Whether there's life after death or not doesn't change the fact that we still have to deal with life today. As Camus said, one must imagine Sisyphus happy rolling his rock up that friggin hill—"

"Right on!" the Camus student exclaimed, to everyone's astonishment. *"The struggle to the heights is enough to make life worth living!"*

Jordan liked his Camus student. "What do you plan to do when you graduate from high school?" he asked the strapping young existentialist.

"I want to practice criminal law like my father," he proudly boasted.

"Then you should read *The Fall.* Camus's protagonist was a lawyer."

"Yes, I know. I read it; but it's too deep for me. My father said he didn't get it until he turned forty. But I'm going to read it again. What about you, Mr. Hansen; did you get what Camus was saying with *The Fall?*"

"I agree with your father," Jordan said, with a wry snicker.

On his drive home he thought about the French philosopher whose book *The Myth of Sisyphus* he devoured in grade twelve. It was a bizarre coincidence that his students should be talking about the meaning of life after the dream he just had, and in the back of his mind he suspected that Elmer had something to do with his day; but he didn't give it any more significance until Monday morning when he overheard a teacher talking to another teacher about the near-death experience that her husband had during his quadruple bypass surgery. "It changed his life," she said.

"In what way?" the older teacher asked, over coffee in the staff room.

"He never used to believe in that kind of stuff. Now he's chatting on the Internet with people who've had near-death experiences. He's not the same man, Doris. He's changed. And he's much easier to live with now."

Doris laughed. "That's a good thing, Karen. I've read about how these kinds of experiences can change a person's personality..."

69

Jordan wanted to join in the conversation, but fear held him back; and that night he had another dream that tilled his mind even more. He was sitting in the back row of a large lecture hall filled with men and women listening to a short man wearing a dark beret with a southern accent talking about personality—

"In itself, personality does not exist" said the man whose southern drawl sounded very familiar. "Personality is a highly evolved unit of consciousness designed by nature for the evolution of the soul of man. Soul uses the human personality to gain life experience, because only through experience can the soul become whole. Soul is a spark of divine consciousness, and man is not complete until he realizes his divine nature; but soul is trapped in life until man refines his personality. Personality is a matrix of the positive and negative consciousness of life, and the consciousness of life is the energy that man needs to grow into the wholeness of his being; but the human personality believes that it is separate from the soul, and it may even deny the existence of soul altogether. Quite often personality believes that it is the only self we have, and when the body dies it dies with the body; but this belief does not stop the soul from growing. On the contrary, this belief has the opposite effect of what people would expect, because it concentrates the consciousness of one's experience and the soul grows much more quickly. Let's take atheists, for example. They live their life with more intensity because they believe this life is all they have, and they concentrate the life force and grow in their spiritual nature much more quickly than most people. This is a curious paradox, and it would shock the non-believer; but this is all part of the Divine Plan of God. I have one more thing I would like to say before you return to your life. Life will always be empty until you create the right kind of personality to free yourself from your lower nature and become a whole person; that's the only way you will ever beat the system and win the final game of life—"

"*That's Elmer!*" Jordan shouted in the darkness of his bedroom, and then he realized that it was just another dream...

16. Plato's Cave

Elmer was in Jordan's dreams now. He didn't know what was happening, and it really began to get on his nerves. He brooded all day long, which was something his father used to do five or six times a month, and then he took the bull by the horns and drove straight to Elmer's house and knocked on his door—

"You're early. My lawn doesn't need cutting yet," Elmer said.

Jordan couldn't tell which Elmer was speaking, but he didn't really care. "I don't know what's going on, but I have to get to the bottom of this!"

"Bottom of what?" Elmer asked. He had a glint in his eyes, but not enough to give him away; but it didn't matter to Jordan which Elmer was speaking.

"You were in my dreams last night, Elmer. I have to know what's going on. May I come in and talk with you?" he said, in one quick breath.

"Sure," Elmer said, and stepped aside for Jordan to enter. He invited him to sit at the kitchen table and then he put on the coffee pot. Jordan wanted a cigarette, but he didn't want to jeopardize his opportunity. Elmer sat down, and with a smile on his face, which looked more wizened than usual, said, "What's on your mind, Jordan?"

"That's just it, I don't know. I think my mind's playing tricks on me, and I want to know if you have anything to do with it."

"Of course I do," Elmer frankly admitted.

"*You do?*" Jordan said, ambushed by Elmer's answer.

"Yes. I'm tilling the soil of your mind, Jordan. That's my job."

"Job? What job?" Jordan asked, still shaken by Elmer's candor.

"I told you, I'm the Wayshower. It's my job to help souls find their way out of the prison of their own mind. It's never occurred to you that your mind is a prison, has it?" Elmer asked, and got up to get the coffee mugs.

"No," Jordan replied, still adjusting to Elmer's frankness.

"Well it is," Elmer said, placing the mugs on the table. He sat down and rested his arms on the table and gazed into Jordan's eyes, and Jordan knew he meant business. "Think of the mind as a multi-dimensioned matrix of reality; but all these separate dimensions are made of the same fabric of the mind to create the illusion of a separate personality. As different as these dimensions may appear to be, they are separate aspects of the same matrix of mental stuff; and my job is to help lost souls find their way out of the matrix of their mind. You see, Jordan; not every person is trapped by the same mental stuff. Every soul creates its own reality and calls it personality; that's what makes everyone different. But when a soul has evolved enough to move on to the final stage of evolution it has to find the Wayshower to show them the way out of the mental world, just like you found me."

"But I wasn't looking for you," Jordan said, as Elmer got up for the coffee.

"You miss the point, Jordan," he said, pouring the aromatic Columbian blend into Jordan's mug. "You're not one self, but two. Actually, you're only one self that has been split in two by the natural process of evolution; and now it's time to reconcile your lower self with your higher self. This is your problem. You're ready to complete what nature cannot finish, but your lower self refuses to be reconciled with your higher self, and I've got my work cut out for me."

Elmer filled his own mug and put the pot back and sat down. Jordan was in deep thought. Everything he said made sense, in its own way; but Jordan had to adjust to Elmer's framework of reality, and he wasn't quite sure what to say.

"Are you saying that I'm a prisoner of my own mind? Have I got that right?"

"Yes," Elmer said, as he stirred his coffee.

"And you're trying to free me from the prison of my mind?"

"BINGO!" Elmer exclaimed.

Jordan fell silent. He drank his coffee, wanting desperately to light a cigarette, and Elmer waited patiently for him to put it all together. "This is really happening to me, isn't it?" Jordan said, fighting his craving for a smoke.

"Yes, but don't tell anyone," Elmer said, with an ironic smile.

"*Who would believe me?*" Jordan snickered.

"No-one," Elmer said, his eyes now shining with love. "People don't want to be seen to be different from the status quo, so they shy away from those that break away. The status quo is the great conformer. It keeps soul trapped in the exoteric stage of evolution. But when soul outgrows the status quo and is ready for the Gnostic Way, it has to fight all those conforming little forces that refuse to let it go. This is natural. It's like a mother seeing her child off to university. She knows she has to let her child go, but she doesn't want to see her leave. In like manner, life knows that soul has to make its own way in the world just as the child going to university, but it's hard for Mother Nature to let soul go back home to God; that's why soul has difficulty breaking away from the status quo. *Capisce,* now?"

Jordan grimaced at the word *capisce*, but he couldn't help but think of his own departure from home; he couldn't wait to leave. "What do you mean by status quo?"

"The many matrixes of the mind," Elmer said.

"What does that mean?" Jordan asked.

"Look out there, Jordan. There are so many dimensions of human expression—science, religion, politics, taxidermy—every conceivable matrix of human expression. Restaurants, golf courses, and vacation getaways; art galleries, movie theaters, social media, computer games, porn sites, and every imaginable expression to satisfy society's every need; whatever you want, it's out there. These are all separate matrixes of the same mental stuff, and no one can break away from the exoteric circle of evolution until life makes them ready for the endgame."

"But how do you know when someone's ready?" Jordan asked.

"I'm the Wayshower, aren't I?" Elmer said, and laughed.

"That doesn't mean anything to me. How do you know when someone is ready for the endgame?" Jordan insisted, with genuine curiosity.

"Fair enough. You know you're ready when you come to a dead end in your life. Nature has taken you as far as it can, and it's up to you to complete the rest of the journey to the wholeness of your true self. You try to make the most of your life, but there's always something missing. You don't know what's missing, but you feel the emptiness in your soul; and it's this emptiness that calls you to the Gnostic Way. And the emptier you feel, the more ready you are for the secret way of life. That's every soul's dilemma. There are no exceptions. Soul flounders in despair, and life seems meaningless and absurd; but that's just another matrix of the mind with the illusion of no exit, just as that other French philosopher expressed it in his play *No Exit*. But didn't Plato say long ago that the prisoners in the cave need someone who has escaped to show them the way to freedom?"

Jordan had heard of Plato's cave from Maria's brother Peter, who told him he was seeking someone to show him the way out; but Jordan always thought Peter was a flake and never took him seriously. "Are you saying I'm a prisoner of my mind like a prisoner in Plato's cave?" he asked, with a twinge of conscience.

"BINGO!" Elmer said, slapping the table with his hand.

Startled for a moment, Jordan sat back to compose himself; and when he felt sure of himself, he said, "And you're going to show me the way out?"

"Bingo again," Elmer said, and laughed.

"Is this why I'm having these strange experiences?"

"I'm just tilling the soil of your mind, Jordan," Elmer said, with a straight face.

"You're freaking me out, that's what you're doing," Jordan said, now really craving a cigarette; but he didn't dare. He had to get all he could out of Elmer while the getting was good. "How long are you going to till my mind?" he asked.

"As long as it takes."

"How long will that be?"

"Until you commit to the endgame."

"And how do I do that?" Jordan asked, with a puzzled stare.

"I'll let you know when and how," Elmer said, and went over to his hat rack on the wall by the back door where he hung his many hats and put on his black beret and adjusted it carefully for Jordan to see. "I feel like a different person with every hat I wear. I like this one. It makes me feel free and debonair. Okay, Jordan; I have another lecture to attend to. I'll see you Thursday when you do my yard."

"What?" Jordan stammered, stunned by Elmer's revelation.

"I'll see you next Thursday," Elmer repeated, and shook Jordan's hand. Jordan felt energy flow from Elmer's hand into his body, and he didn't want to let go; but Elmer smiled, and said, "That should do for now."

Jordan drove home feeling like he wasn't losing his mind after all, but there was something definitely going on; and rather than drink himself to sleep as he often did, he stayed awake most of the night trying to make sense of his life.

17. Peter Augustino

Jordan didn't make the connection until a few days later while sitting in his classroom in Hampton High. It was the second week of the new school year and his third day supply teaching for the teacher who flew to Vancouver for her twin brother's funeral, and he was beginning to get comfortable again.

The money was excellent, not to mention safe and secure, and the work was nothing compared to the physical effort he had to make mowing half a dozen lawns or snowplowing the same to add up to one day's wages teaching school, and the thought began to play on his mind that he should apply for a fulltime position, but then he cast it out because he had vowed to be his own man.

That's why he walked away from his profession. Primed by half a dozen beer, he threatened his wife that he felt like packing it in—

"Pack what in?" Sharon snapped back, in that sarcastic tone that cut Jordan to the bone. "Teaching? You have it so good now you'd die out there on your own. You talk like you're your own man, Jordan; but you've never been your own man. Your banker put you through university and you've been on the gravy train every since. You're just another civil servant sucking on the government teat like the rest of us!"

Sharon cut him so deeply that Jordan began to brood; and because he didn't' have the courage to pack it in like he boasted, his wife rubbed it into his face every chance she could to keep him in his place, and he drank more to kill his shame.

But regardless how much he drank he had to look at himself in the mirror every day, and he began to loathe himself for betraying Maria and his children; and the day after his wife robbed him of his final shred of dignity he was trimming his goatee, which he sported from his first year of university, when his face began to morph before his eyes and a strange demonic face that looked like his own stared back at him with the most contemptuous sneer he had ever seen, and he jumped back in horror and dropped his straight razor to the floor.

He shut his eyes and took a deep breath and forced himself to look into the mirror, and he was relieved to see his own face again; but he was so horrified by that other face that he never wanted to see it again, and he shaved off his goatee and saw his old face again for the first time since he went to university, and as he stared at his old self he felt alive again and an unbelievable surge of courage possessed him—

"Fuck it!" he exclaimed, and he submitted his resignation to the principal and told his wife he wanted a divorce, and at the end of the term packed his things and moved to Georgian Bay, Ontario to become his own man.

He did his research and started his own business in Hampton Beach, and on the advice of his bank manager whom he befriended in the clubhouse at *Hampton Golf and Country Club* after several rounds of golf he applied to the Ontario Teachers College for certification to supply teach in Ontario so he would be better qualified for the bank loan that he would need to buy the house he was leasing.

As he waited for his students to do an assignment that Miss Ambrose had left for them, he pondered his talk with Elmer and his ex-brother-in-law Peter Augustino popped into his mind, and he suddenly realized what he meant when he said that he was going away to look for someone to show him the way out of Plato's cave—

Maria's bachelor brother, who was four years older than his favorite sister, was different. Jordan thought he was a flake, but he never let his feelings known to Maria and her family. Peter was like no one Jordan had ever met. He was inside himself so deep that not even his favorite sister Maria could reach him, and he only let you into his life if he felt like it, which was only so far and not often; and he never let Jordan in far enough to see the real Peter Augustino, but he always teased him.

Peter came and went when he pleased, seemingly on a whim, never letting anyone know where he was going or when he was coming back. He would be gone for months at a time without a word to anyone, telling his family that he was going to "Sanctuary," and twice he went away for three year periods; and every time he went away he came back a little more inscrutable and mysterious. But when he came home from his first three-year stint to this place he called "Sanctuary," he was so different that his family did not know what to make of him. He no longer ate meat, nor did he drink alcohol, not even a glass of wine for dinner, which was a sacred family tradition; and because he had no interest in women he was suspected of being gay, but he wasn't. He had taken a personal vow of celibacy for self-discipline.

"Where were you for the last three years?" Jordan asked.

"Working my way out of Plato's cave," Peter replied, with a wry smile.

"Pardon?" Jordan said, shaking his head at Peter's cryptic nature.

"I went on my quest for my true self," Peter amplified, and chuckled.

His laugh unnerved Jordan. "So, where'd you go?"

"I went to Sanctuary?" Peter replied.

"Where's that, Tibet? India? Where'd you go, Peter?"

"In here," Peter said, pointing to his heart.

"You're really strange, you know that?"

"Anyone called to a higher purpose is strange, Jordan; but you wouldn't know that, would you? You're so invested in yourself you can't see the wood for the trees. But one day even Jordan Hansen will be called by Soul, and then you'll understand where I'm coming from."

"Called by Soul?" Jordan said, befuddled by Peter's strange remark. "Called for what?" he asked, and lit another cigarette to keep himself grounded.

"To climb out of Plato's cave," Peter said, with a snicker that made Jordan grimace. "Look, Jordan; there are three stages to man's evolution through life," he explained, in his serious philosophical voice that always threatened Jordan. "The first stage gave birth to man's reflective self. This is where the majority of mankind finds itself. But man has a teleological imperative to realize his higher nature, which he can't do on his own because he's trapped by his lower self. Man is a prisoner in Plato's cave, if you will; and he needs help to break free of his lower nature. Socrates, who was Plato's teacher and mouthpiece in Plato's writing, addresses man's predicament with his allegory of the cave in Plato's dialogue *The Republic*. Man is a prisoner of his own consciousness, just as the prisoners in Plato's metaphorical cave are unaware of the real world outside their world of shadows and reflections; and the only way to free oneself from the prison of his own consciousness is to find a teacher of the Way. You want to know where I go when I go to Sanctuary; well, to be quite frank with you, I go in search of a Gnostic teacher to show me the way out of Plato's cave. That's what I've been doing for the last three years. *Capisce*, now?"

Again, Jordan grimaced. He was totally puzzled. "What's a Gnostic teacher?"

"Someone who knows the way out of Plato's cave," Peter repeated; and to get Jordan off the hook, he said, "Let's have another game of chess..."

Peter Augustino was his own man. He never held down a job for more than a year or two, but he never seemed to worry, living as though today was his last; and as much as Jordan tried to like Peter for his wife's sake, he couldn't. Something about Peter Augustino got under Jordan's skin, and it unnerved him.

"Mr. Hansen," one of his grade eleven students called, summoning him back to the moment. "What do we do with our paper when we're finished?"

"Sign your name and hand it in for Miss Ambrose. She'll be marking them, if she's back tomorrow. If not, you'll have the pleasure of my grading system; and I promise you, I don't make concessions."

As he waited for his students to finish their paper, he was struck by the thought like a bolt out of the blue that Elmer was Peter's Gnostic teacher! He didn't know why that thought came to him, but he just *knew* he was right, and he shuddered.

His legs began to tremble. Everything that Elmer had revealed to him about Plato's cave was connected with his ex-brother-in-law Peter Augustino, whom Jordan could never figure out; but now—Jordan froze in astonishment. The realization was overwhelming, and he had to have a cigarette to calm his nerves.

He told his class he had to step out for a few minutes, and he lit a cigarette the moment he stepped outside the school. *"Maybe he wasn't so strange after all,"* he thought to himself, as he puffed on his cigarette. *"What the hell's going on?"*

The last time Jordan saw Peter was the year before he abandoned Maria and the children when he drove from Oakville to visit them on his way to Vancouver where he was going to look for work and perhaps settle down, but Peter said something to Jordan over a game of chess that puzzled him at the time but was as clear as a bell in retrospect: "The seeds that you planted in your marriage have sprouted, grown, and born wonderful fruit in Mark and Lisa; but you're dying on the vine, Jordan. I'll give you one year before you make your move."

A chill shot through Jordan's body. "What move?"

Peter smiled that smile that Jordan hated, but he was too afraid to ask what he meant; but now it was so clear that his whole body began to burn with the searing shame of his betrayal. He puffed on his cigarette to calm his nerves, but he went back to his classroom knowing that he had condemned himself to the depths of his own private hell when he agreed to stay the night with the woman who broke up his marriage, and he would give anything to have his old life back again...

18. The Bringer of Enlightenment

Peter worked for a year and nine months for his uncle Frank on different building sites in Oakville and Milton, and he saved every cent he could to go on his quest for a spiritual teacher that would lead him out of Plato's cave of shadows and reflections, teachers like his Holiness the Dalai Lama that he had placed on his pared-down list of teachers that he was determined to look up; but he left himself open to serendipity which always seemed to play a role in Peter's life.

He packed his travelling back-pack with the bare necessities and flew to New Delhi, India; and from there he took a bus to Dharamsala where the exiled spiritual leader of the Tibetan people his Holiness the Dalai Lama made his headquarters after China invaded his country, and he tried to make an appointment with his officious secretary but was told that his Holiness' calendar was full for five and six months at a time and it was impossible to fit him in, but Peter was persistent—

"I'm going to come every day until his Holiness sees me," he told the secretary, and he got a hotel room in Dharamsala and came every day for a week, waiting where he was conspicuous; but on the eighth day he was told by a member of the staff that his Holiness would squeeze him into his busy schedule, and he was led to the first of three waiting rooms and frisked by a Tibetan man. Half an hour later Peter was led to a second waiting room and searched by a much more serious Indian solider, and then he was taken to another waiting room and sat beside a monk who was so nervous he kept cracking his knuckles. Peter was nervous too.

The monk was called away, and when he came out ten minutes later he had the most radiant smile on his face and bowed to Peter in a gesture of love, wishing him the same blessing that he had received from his Holiness the Dalai Lama. Peter was led into the meeting room, which was decorated in bright Tibetan colors and had a statue of Avalokiteshvara that Peter learned from the monk he met in the waiting room was the Buddhist representative of compassion. He also learned from the monk that some Tibetans including himself considered the Dalai Lama to be the manifestation of the deity Avalokiteshvara, though his Holiness always referred to himself as a humble Buddhist monk which Peter felt the moment he met him.

Peter bowed reverently, and his Holiness bowed back with a twinkle in his eyes and the biggest smile on his bespectacled happy face. Peter gave him his hand, and the Dalai Lama took his hand with both of his and held it long enough to make Peter comfortable, and then the Dalai Lama broke into giddy laughter.

The Dalai Lama was famous for his laughter, and he laughed for no apparent reason; but it was infectious, and Peter laughed with him. It was like his lungs had been filled with laughing gas, and he felt giddy and light-headed; but he had come to ask the eminent Buddhist teacher one question, and when their laughter subsided Peter took a deep breath and said, "Your Holiness, can your teaching lead me out of Plato's cave of spiritual ignorance and complacency?"

The Dalai Lama's expression changed. "Only you can do that."

"How?" Peter asked, surprised by his quick answer; for sure Peter thought he would be asked about Plato's cave, but apparently there was no need.

"You must practice compassion," the Dalai Lama answered without a flicker of hesitation, in his serious sonorous voice that spoke for centuries of Buddhist wisdom. "Must practice compassion every day," said his Holiness. "Compassion morning, noon, and night. Compassion for family, friends, strangers, all enemies, especially enemies; and compassion for animals, birds, fish, insects, plants, all life; and self too. Very important you practice compassion for self," he stressed, touching Peter's arm and smiling. "Compassion leads to purification. Purification leads to enlightenment. Enlightenment is freedom from attachment. Non-attachment is emptiness of mind. Emptiness of mind is Nirvana. Compassion is the path to *moksha*. When you have *moksha*, you have no more ignorance. No more complacency. You free."

Peter was writing the Dalai Lama's words in his notebook, and when he looked up he said, "Your Holiness, do Buddhists believe in God?"

The Dalai Lama smiled, but his voice still spoke for the ages: "If God is Truth, or ultimate Reality, there is a God according to Buddhism. If God is the Creator and is all-knowing and all-merciful, then Buddhists do not believe in God. Buddhists believe in self-creation and karma. All self is one. All sentient beings have Buddha seed. All Buddha seeds have potential for enlightenment as long as there is mind or consciousness. To achieve enlightenment you must practice compassion and wisdom. Compassion and wisdom lead to *moksha*, perfect enlightenment."

"What is perfect enlightenment?" Peter asked.

"It is mental state of complete purification. It is state of suchness, emptiness, interdependent relationship of all phenomena," his Holiness explained, with a serious look that let Peter know the importance of complete purification. "When you purify self and understand interrelatedness of all phenomena, you realize ultimate state of perfect enlightenment. It is simple," said his Holiness, and instantly broke into giddy laughter at the irony of his imperative.

Peter caught the irony and broke into laughter also, realizing in that moment why the Dalai Lama laughed so much. "So I simply have to be compassionate and wise to become enlightened?" Peter said, with a straight face.

"Yes, very simple," the Dalai Lama said again, and broke into another spurt of giddy laughter like it was a great cosmic joke.

"Of course it is," said Peter, and joined in the Dalai Lama's profound sense of humor; but seeing that his time was up by the glance his aid gave him, he looked into the Dalai Lama's eyes and bowed in deep respect. "Thank you, your Holiness. I am very grateful for your time. I will practice compassion and become very wise."

His Holiness broke into laughter again, and Peter had to join him; and then the humble Buddhist monk bowed much lower than before, which made Peter feel very special; and he left the first teacher on his list with a smile on his face and lightness in his heart, and the following day he began to search out another teacher that he heard about by chance from his seat companion on the bus to Dharamsala.

With the little English that the man spoke, he got across to Peter that a man from the mountains had been coming to his little village for the past year to bring them enlightenment. Peter wrote down the name of the village in his notebook and made a point to seek this teacher out; and in the morning he took a taxi from Dharamsala to his travelling companion's village, and to his delight he found a thickly cropped black haired man who looked to be no more than thirty-five or forty—which Peter thought much too young to be a bringer of enlightenment—with a short dark beard wearing a knee-length maroon robe holding a big walking stick and surrounded by a crowd of people at his feet as he spoke to them in their native tongue. Peter grabbed his backpack and paid the taxi driver and walked over to the crowd and sat on the ground to listen to the man with the big stick.

A strange thing happened as Peter walked over to the villagers caught in rapturous attention to the bringer of enlightenment whose face now looked vaguely familiar; he felt like he was being drawn into a magnetic field of enormous spiritual energy, and with every step he took he felt himself being pulled deeper and deeper into himself, and he could not explain the feeling that he had met this man before.

He could not understand a single word the man said, but after a few minutes of listening to his deep and powerful voice, which created an image in Peter's mind of a roaring waterfall, the man turned and fixed his gaze on Peter, and the instant their eyes met Peter's world was thrown into confusion—

All the love in the universe poured out of the man's coal black eyes into Peter's famished soul, and he was so intoxicated by love that he jumped to his feet and started dancing in wild ecstatic joy!

Peter danced and danced in abandoned rapture and everyone understood that he had been blessed with the Master's Gaze, which was known to them as the *Tiwaja*, and they all stared in awe because they knew what the blessing meant; but Peter had no idea and he just danced and danced like a crazy fool of God...

19. The Man with the Big Stick

Peter was too confused to go after the man who gave him the Master's Gaze, so he managed to find accommodations in the village. One of the men in the crowd offered him a bed for the night, and the next morning the man's wife offered him something to eat and Peter wanted to pay them.

"The Master has blessed you," said his host, with reverence in his voice as he gently touched Peter's arm. "Your blessing is our blessing. Go up the village road north. That is where the Master comes from. You may find him there."

Peter did as he was told, and true to the villager's words he found the man in the maroon robe walking towards him with his big walking stick.

He was on his way to the village to bring enlightenment, and Peter stopped and waited for him, feeling his powerful energy as he approached. The man raised his hand in greeting, and when they met he looked into Peter's eyes and he felt the power of the Master's Gaze once more and swooned in the fury of God's love; but the man put his hand on Peter's shoulder and he felt a calm wash over him.

"You have come far, Peter," said the man.

"You know my name?"

"And the purpose of your visit. Come, let us find a place to sit and talk," said the man, and they walked over to a little grove of trees.

The man leaned his big stick on a tree and sat down and leaned his back on the trunk and shut his eyes. Peter sat at his feet, and with his eyes still shut the bringer of enlightenment quietly said, "Ask me what you will."

"Anything?" Peter said nervously.

"'I say what I mean and I mean what I say,' the man replied, quoting from *Alice in Wonderland*. "You have earned the privilege. Ask."

Peter had only one question, which for some reason he felt needed no explanation: "Can you show me the way out of Plato's cave?"

"You need not have journeyed so far to learn the secrets of the Gnostic Way," the bringer of enlightenment responded, his eyes wide open. "Socrates reveals the secret way in Plato's Dialogues. As you know, Plato's cave is an elaborate metaphor for the mind of man, and liberation from the mind is man's final journey home to God. You are correct to feel that the Laughing Master's way will only lead you deeper into the Cosmic Mind and not to the worlds of God beyond the Mental Plane where you become one with your divine nature; that is why you were blessed by the merciful law of synchronicity to find your way to me. When the student is ready, the Master must appear. The path you seek is the Gnostic teaching 'whose high endeavors are an inward light/That makes the path before him always bright,' as the English poet Wordsworth expressed the secret way of life in his immortal poem *Character of the Happy Warrior*—"

Peter leaned forward to ask something, but something stopped him.

"Socrates taught the secret teachings of the Gnostic Way," the man continued, his black eyes burning like hot coals that warmed Peter's heart with God's love, just like the love he received from a mystic carpenter long ago on his uncle's building site. "Did not Socrates teach that only through death can soul find its way out of the cave of ignorance and complacency? The death that Socrates speaks of is the death of the little self. *'I deem that the true disciple of philosophy is likely to be misunderstood by other men; they do not perceive that he is ever pursuing death and dying,'* said Socrates in Plato's *Phaedo*. You have come all this way to India to confirm your understanding of Plato's philosophy and the noble path of virtue that can be found in the heart of life like the bee that gathers the sweet nectar of the flower, and I assure you Peter Augustino that this sweet nectar of goodness is the clarity at the heart of work, regardless of one's profession. Be true to yourself and never cut corners in what you do; that is the way out of Plato's cave. Now go into the world and practice the art of conscious dying, and when you are ready you will find your way to the Wayshower who will guide you on the rest of your journey home to God."

"The Wayshower?" Peter asked, never hearing that word before.

"Yes. He is in North America. He will come to you when you are ready," and with that the man grabbed his walking stick and began to walk away, but he turned and raised his hand, and said, *"May the blessing be."*

Peter felt the love of the Master's blessing, and all the fear he had of finding his way out of Plato's cave disappeared, and he started walking back to the village. The man could not have been more than twenty feet away when Peter realized who he was, but when he went to call his name he had vanished into thin air!

20. Keeper of the Tomb

From India Peter went to Australia and worked on a sheep station for two months for room and board to get his yen for Australia out of his system, and from there he flew to Paris and went to Fontainebleau-Avon where the man who gave him the key to Sanctuary with his teaching of "work on oneself" was buried, and he placed a single yellow rose on his gravestone as he had promised. "Thank you, Mr. G," he said, with tears in his eyes; and then he hiked his way to Turkey to find a Sufi teacher that would teach him the art of conscious dying. But he had to go to Konya first to see Rumi's tomb and the dervish museum, as well as the much more spare building that was said to house the remains of Rumi's teacher, the mysterious Shams of Tabriz; so Peter played it by ear and let his "Oracle" guide him in his search.

It was Ramadan, and Peter did as everyone and fasted from sunup to sundown; and he spent his first few days contemplating in Shams' tomb, quietly reading Rumi's poetry which spoke to his heart from the day he was introduced to it by the mystic carpenter Framer John on his uncle Frank's building site; and around eight every evening he went to the same restaurant and waited for the call from the minaret to eat, and then he would order a bottle of water with his lentil soup and meal.

For the longest time Peter thought it was his Canadian pronunciation, because when he ordered water in Turkish, which the keeper of Shams' tomb had taught him precisely how to pronounce, he would draw a little crowd from the kitchen to watch the waiter take his order. Peter wasn't aware of it, but every time he ordered water (*su*), his pronunciation made it sound like he was ordering the secret of the universe (*sir*), and all the staff would break into joyous laughter and then went about their duties. They did this every night of his stay in Konya, and Peter was none the wiser until a Sufi friend back in Toronto revealed the source of their laughter and put Peter wise to the tomb keeper's playful Nasruddin-like sense of humor.

Whenever Peter went to contemplate in the tomb of the man who ravished Rumi's heart with the devastating love of God, he would sit on the floor or lean his back to a wall to read Rumi's verse; but the keeper of the tomb would politely align Peter's body. Peter would thank him politely, and the keeper of the tomb would smile and say, "Without love, the garden of life will wither and die."

The keeper of Shams' tomb was a broad, heavyset man of medium height, with flashing dark eyes that read Peter's heart at a glance. His dark hair was long but his beard was short, and some days he wore a floppy, wide-brimmed hat. He spoke perfect English without a British accent, as well as several other languages, and his voice was deep and resonant, and he smelled of jasmine. Peter felt good when he contemplated in Shams' tomb, and he struck a friendship with the keeper. He looked up from his book one day and said, "Nasruddin's quite the teacher, isn't he?"

The keeper's face lit up. "What would we do without Nasruddin? He is the spiritual embodiment of the Gnostic Way!"

"You mean the Sufi Path," Peter corrected.

"The Sufi Path is the Gnostic Way," said the keeper.

"I never knew that," Peter said.

"It stands to reason, does it not?" the keeper replied, in perfect English.

Peter thought for a moment. "Yes. The Sufi Path speaks the way to God; ergo, it must *know* the Way. But then—"

"Exactly," said the keeper, reading Peter's thoughts. "The Gnostic Way is the way of all ways in the garden of life. It is the secret way back home to God."

Peter smiled at the keeper's wisdom and wanted to take advantage of his new friendship. He glanced at the passage he had underscored in his book on the exploits of the remarkable

Sufi trickster and asked the keeper what he thought of the story of Nasruddin's conundrum—

"Nasruddin was in a tavern all night. When he left, it was four in the morning and he wandered about the town aimlessly. A policeman stopped and asked him. 'Why are you out wandering the streets in the middle of the night?' Nasruddin replied, 'If I knew the answer to that question, I would have been home long ago.' I think he's talking about states of consciousness here, don't you?"

"Perfectly," said the keeper of the tomb. "The tavern is life; and soul drinks of life and gets inebriated on life. In its inebriation, soul loses direction to its home. Nasruddin's home is the House of God, and he is telling the seeker that to find the House of God soul must sober up. And how does soul sober up from life?"

"By living the Sufi Path, I would think," Peter answered.

"That is one way. But the Gnostic Way is best," replied the keeper.

"Why?" Peter asked.

"The Gnostic Way is the way of the *knowing* heart."

"*Knowing* heart?" Peter said, with a frown. "I've never heard that expression before. What is the *knowing* heart?"

"Conscious love," replied the keeper.

"Isn't all love conscious?" Peter asked.

"Love is conscious when the lover knows God with his heart," said the keeper, in a voice that sounded to Peter like it came from heaven, "and it is not conscious when the lover does not know God with his heart. Gnosis of God is conscious love, and the path to know God is the way of the *knowing* heart; ergo, the Gnostic Way.

"I have fallen in love twice in my life," said Peter. "I knew I was in love with the women I fell in love with. Was my love for them not conscious love?"

"Conscious love transcends romantic love," said the keeper, the sound of his words tasting like sweet honey.

"Conscious love is pure and unconditional. It does not judge, and it has no expectations. Conscious love just IS!"

"I am in love; ergo, I am," Peter said, and broke into laughter.

The keeper of the tomb laughed with Peter. "There is more wisdom in what you say than you realize. What is it you seek in Konya? Are you here for Ramadan, or do you wish to find a teacher?"

"Both," Peter answered.

"What kind of teacher do you seek?"

"One who will teach me the art of dying before dying."

"Ahhh, the conscious death!"

"Maybe if I learn how to die before I die I will learn how to love more consciously," Peter said, and broke into laughter again.

The keeper enjoyed Peter's humor, and smiled with joy; then in a serious voice, he said, "Your thirst for the secret of the universe is greater than your body's thirst for water. Go back to your studies of Plato. Socrates will give you what you seek to solve the riddle of your life. *'And what is purification but the separation of soul from the body, the habit of soul gathering and collecting herself into herself,'* said the Gnostic Master. With the purifying power of virtue, Socrates revealed the sacred art of dying before dying. The noble virtues are the way out of your conundrum."

Peter looked into the keeper's eyes, and they were so clear and deep that they seemed to know all the wisdom of God. "Who are you?" Peter asked.

"Who would you like me to be," replied the keeper.

"Shams of Tabriz," Peter said, jokingly.

"Your wish is my command," said the keeper, and began to pirouette with his hand in the air; and when he stopped spinning he looked into Peter's eyes and his whole world fell apart as it did with the bringer of enlightenment in the little village in India. The love that poured out of Shams' eyes ravished

Peter's heart, and he started spinning like a whirling dervish and was swept away into another world...

21. The Metamorphoses of Peter Augustino

From Turkey Peter went to Italy. He wanted to visit his place of birth, but he did not announce his visit to his extended family in Reggio Calabria. He traveled like a tourist, just to get the feel of his native country that had encoded his personality; and when he had soaked up all the ancestral consciousness that he could from the people of his native land, he knew what he had to do to live the Gnostic Way—*he had to die to that part of himself that kept him from being his true self!*

When Peter was whirling like a dervish in the tomb of the great Shams of Tabriz who ravished his heart with the love of God, he was swept away to the Golden Wisdom Temple of Sakapori on the Causal Plane where he met the guardian of the temple who just happened to be the same mystic keeper of Sham's tomb, and with that same ironic smile he granted Peter the privilege of viewing the Holy Book of Gnostic Wisdom that glowed in a magnificent golden light.

The light poured out of the Holy Book in beams of sacred knowledge, and as he looked into the light the ancient wisdom of the secret way of life quenched his thirsty soul, and he saw the endless journey of souls flowing like a great river of eternal life through the minerals of the world and on through the flora and fauna of nature's garden and up the ladder of all creature life to the birth of the reflective self of man in the higher primates where the journey of the self to the higher worlds of God continued from one life to the next until man was ready for the Gnostic Way in the final stage of evolution to his divine nature; and the light shone with such brilliance that he saw the lowly self of man metamorphose into a God-realized Soul like a lowly caterpillar transforming itself into a magnificent butterfly, and Peter knew that he had witnessed the mystery of life's essential purpose in the Divine Plan of God.

The guardian of the temple tapped Peter on the shoulder. "If you drink any more of the bliss of God you will upset your spiritual balance. You have what you came for, Peter; now work out the details and forge your own path to God, as every soul must. Come, we must return to my tomb," he said, with a wink...

Peter left Konya with a new and enlightened purpose, and he traveled to the ancient village of Panettieri in the boot of Italy to see the house where he was born; and he learned why he felt the way he did about his Italian heritage. The spirit of *la miseria* still lingered in Calabria, and Peter understood why his parents were the way they were and could now forgive them for their stubborn pride and superstition; and from Italy he went to Mount Athos in the Greek Isles and made a pilgrimage to Megisti Lavra, the oldest monastery on the Holy Mountain where an aged monk sanctified by half a century of prayer and contemplation helped put his Christian demons to rest with a simple Jesus prayer the monk gave to Peter to recite every day for the rest of his life, and then he went to Athens to walk on the same ground that his beloved Socrates walked; and then he back-packed through Europe picking up odd jobs here and there to help pay his way, and his first day in England serendipity brought him to a village market where he chanced upon a leather-bound volume of *Plato's Dialogues* in a book stall set up by a retired librarian whose love of literature excited Peter's fascination, and he devoured Plato with new passion and resolved the Gnostic secret of the noble virtues that helped set him free from the karmic prison of his ancestral roots that had chained him to his *family shadow* that was conceived in *la miseria* of Reggio Calabria where pride and ignorance were still a way of life.

He took one noble virtue to live by each day and forged his own path in the smithy of his soul as he hiked throughout the British Isles, shouting with each breath he took "Welcome O Life!" like Joyce's young hero in *A Portrait of the Artist as a*

Young Man that he read in a Dublin pub, and he saturated himself with the wisdom of those ancient lands that inspired the poet whose Happy Warrior became his ideal, and by the time he returned to his home in Oakville, Ontario three years and two months from the day he left Canada, Peter Augustino was a transformed man.

His family saw the change in Peter when he refused to drink wine at the family dinner, and he tried to explain his strange behavior. "I got tested for allergies in Europe," he lied to his family, to safeguard the secret path. "I break into a rash if I drink alcohol," he said; and the word spread throughout his family that he had become allergic to alcoholic beverages. But try as he may, he could not hide his new Gnostic attitude when dining on his family's home-cooked meals.

It wasn't that Peter no longer drank alcohol and stopped eating meat that perplexed his family, which he explained by telling them that he just wanted to try the vegetarian life to see if it made a difference to his health, he also practiced the devastating technique that he learned from Mr. G of *non-identifying* with the objects of his desire, which included his favorite recipes like his mother's gnocchi, for the Gnostic purpose of transforming the consciousness of his ego self; and the more disciplined he became in the alchemy of *non-identifying* with the objects of his desire, the more he alienated himself from family members, which only gave rise to more suspicion just as Jesus said would happen if he set his hand to the plow and died to his life to find his life, and Peter saw his family on special occasions only; but he had to stop going to regular family functions to not provoke the ancestral *family shadow*, which only alienated him all the more from his close-knit family that could never have enough success in life, and Peter hurt his family unintentionally with his disciplined attitude of detachment from everything his family held dear.

But he went to Winnipeg several times a year to visit his sister Maria, and he stayed for a month and a half to console her when Jordan packed up and left her for the other woman. "I didn't see it coming," she said to Peter through fresh tears. "I know we had a problem, but I didn't expect that."

"I did," Peter said.

"You did?" his sister said, with some surprise.

"Yes," Peter said. "And I told him as much."

"What are you saying, Peter?"

"The last time I came to visit shortly after my long trek to Sanctuary, I told Jordan he had one year at most before he made his move. He didn't know what I was talking about; but this is what I was talking about, sis. I saw it coming long before he pulled the rug out from under you."

"How? I didn't see it. How could you know?"

"I'm very familiar with the male ego, sis. I've been studying it for years, especially in our family and Italian community where men strut like peacocks and women put on airs of being more than what they are, and I know how ego works. Your husband has always been a self-serving egoist from the day you married him, and it was only a matter of time before he flip-flopped."

"Flip-flopped?" Maria said, intrigued by Peter's insight. "What do you mean?"

"I don't know if I can explain it, sis. It has to do with the dynamics of the human personality. It's the Jekyll and Hyde thing. It's very complex."

"I don't care how complex it is, Peter; you have to tell me. I have to know why my husband betrayed us the way he did. It's not enough for him to say we grew apart. That's not good enough. That's a lie. It may be true, but it's a lie Peter. You know what I mean. He hid behind that to hide the truth. I know my husband, and I know we could have worked it out; but he didn't give us a chance. He wasn't himself, Peter. He wanted to move back to Ontario, but he couldn't get a job there; and I wasn't going to move without a transfer. I worked too hard for my career. Jordan was hurting, Peter; I know that. And I think that teacher took advantage of him. That's why he packed his suitcase and moved in with her. 'I'm leaving you,' he said; and the next day he had the nerve to come back to mow the lawn and drink a beer like nothing happened. He took his wedding band off his finger and put it on the table in front of me and Mark and Lisa and said that's how rational people behaved. I couldn't believe my eyes. It was like a scene right out of a French film *noire*—"

Maria broke down. Peter held her in his arms until she stopped crying, and when she was ready Peter took a breath, looked into his sister's beautiful hazel brown eyes swollen from crying, and said: "Maria, what Jordan did was selfish and cold blooded; but that's the nature of the *shadow* self. It has no feelings for anyone but itself. This may not make any sense to you, but it has to do with the Jekyll/Hyde syndrome. Our personality is split in two. The *shadow* is the unconscious part of our personality, and when the personality does a flip-flop the conscious part loses control and the unconscious part called the *shadow* takes over. Jordan took a crippling blow to his ego when he couldn't get the job transfer he wanted to Ontario. He was humbled, Maria; but when you couple his humiliation with your new promotion to a bigger bank and boost in salary his self-image got shattered, and he went into crisis mode to salvage his wounded pride. That's why he flip-flopped. His *shadow* came out and took over his personality to rescue his wounded ego. You said you didn't recognize him after he left you, and neither did Mark and Lisa, like he was a different person; that's because he was a different person. His *shadow* was always hidden and unseen, but when he flip-flopped his *shadow* came out and took over his personality and he became a different person. That's why you and the kids couldn't recognize him. His *shadow* was always there, hidden in his ego-personality; you just couldn't see it, that's all. It takes special sight to see the false *shadow* side of our personality; but I learned how to see the *shadow* every time I went to Sanctuary, so I saw Jordan's *shadow* long before he flip-flopped. That's why your husband and I never saw eye to eye. His false *shadow* self resented me because it couldn't hide from me. I expected him to do something like this, Maria; but I couldn't tell you."

"You could have given me a heads up," Maria said, grabbing Peter's arm.

"There was no point, sis. Jordan's ego was much too intransigent. He thought he had the world by the nuts until it bit him in the ass. The world has its own way of leveling people off, sis; and I promise you, one day he's going to learn that he has to play the game of life by the rules whether he likes it or not."

"I'll never get over what he did to us," Maria said, fighting back more tears. "He's still the father of my children, but I can't help thinking that my whole marriage was a lie. Peter, do you think my marriage was a lie?'

"Not for you, it wasn't. You did not marry in white, and you gave your husband your truest self; but try as he may, he couldn't exhaust your virtue with his selfish ego. You planted good seeds, sis; but his selfish *shadow* was the bad seed that he couldn't stop from choking the virtue of your marriage. From what I understand of his family, he got that bad seed from his father; and, at the risk of saying something I shouldn't, I suspect his bad seed has been passed on to your daughter Lisa."

"No way," Maria said, with a look of fright.

"She's her father's daughter, sis. Mark took after you."

"Maybe," Maria consented, reluctantly. "I just hope there's enough of me in her to fight her father's bad seed, then. My God, it hurts Peter. I never thought I could hurt so much. It hurts so deep my soul aches. Will it ever go away?"

"Time, sis. Just be patient. And whatever you do, try not to let your hurt sour you on life. It'll ruin you if it does. Take the high road, please..."

Peter consoled his sister and niece and nephew, but no amount of comfort could relieve the hurt that Jordan had inflicted upon his wife and children; but Peter knew that one day Jordan's betrayal would come back to haunt him.

22. Chinese Dinner

It was Friday, and when Jordan got home from supply teaching a grade nine class in the Beach he had a couple of beer before driving to the GOLDEN WOK in Carlton for his treat of all-you-can eat Chinese dinner.

He looked forward to his bi-weekly buffet dinners, and he had one last cigarette before entering the restaurant. He ordered a Molson's Canadian and drank it slowly as he reflected on his day at school. He enjoyed his day, except for his thoughts of Peter; and no sooner did Peter enter his mind again, and he grimaced—

"So tell me, Jordan," said Peter Augustino, in that probing tone of voice that Jordan had come to recognize as they played their nightly game of chess whenever Peter visited them in Winnipeg; "why is it so important for you to win all the time?"

"That's the point of the game, isn't it?" he replied.

"Yes, of course; but there's winning and there's winning. You have to win. That's your nature. Why do you have to win all the time?"

Jordan didn't like it when Peter got philosophical, which he seemed to do with everything they talked about, and he found his question intrusive. "I guess I just like to win," he said, and made his move.

Peter studied Jordan's move and then moved his queen. "Everybody likes to win," Peter responded; "but you *have* to win?" They were playing in Jordan's den in the basement, the only room in the house where he was allowed to smoke, and Jordan lit another cigarette to study his next move. "I'm only asking because I'm working on a theory," Peter added.

"What theory?" Jordan asked, taking a long drag of his cigarette.

"The exchange of energies between people," Peter explained.

Jordan shook his head as he often did at Peter and fixed his eyes on the board again. "Give me a minute. I think I've got my next move..."

Jordan moved, and Peter's queen was in danger. Peter studied the board and moved to protect his queen, but he lost it; and Jordan went to the bar fridge in the family room and treated himself to another beer.

Peter couldn't salvage the game, but Jordan didn't know if Peter had deliberately sacrificed his queen. They played again, and Peter won; and Jordan had to play once more for the best of three.

"You didn't answer my question," Peter said, after Jordan moved his pawn. "Why is it so important for you to win all the time?"

"That's the way my father raised me, I guess," Jordan replied in a flippant tone of voice, hoping to dismiss the unnerving subject; but Peter persisted. "Raised you to be a winner, or raised you to *have* to win?"

"What's the difference? Winning is winning."

"No, it's not. When you have to win all the time it means that you have to have something that winning takes from the loser. What do you suppose that certain something is?" Peter asked, with a subtle smile.

"What are you talking about? When you win, you win. That's not complicated, is it? I think you make too much of life, Peter. Life is black and white for me. You win, you lose; that's what life is all about. I try to win all the time because I like to win. That's simple enough..." And the day after Peter left, Jordan was challenged to run the Manitoba Marathon, and just like Peter said, he *had* to win the bet—

Anxious, Jordan dismissed Peter from his mind and went to the buffet table to begin his dinner (to his chagrin, he lost the best of three to Peter that night), and his eyes devoured the huge pile of crab legs; but he started with wonton soup and a plate of various salads and returned to his table. That's when he spotted the ancient looking Oriental man with the braided ponytail and pointed white beard at the adjacent table smiling at him as he set his soup and salad down.

The man was all dressed in white and very slender, with luminous dark eyes, and his face glowed benevolence and goodwill; and he bowed his head in deep respect. *"Bon appetite,"* he said, which sounded strange coming from an Oriental.

"You too," Jordan said, and raised his glass of beer, taking the man to be the owner of the restaurant or an elder relative of one of the all Oriental staff, and then he ladled some hot broth into his mouth enjoying the pure beef flavor.

He felt the Oriental man staring, but he paid no attention and ladled a slippery wonton into his white ceramic spoon and ate it slowly with relish; but the aged Oriental spoke up in a voice that sounded like wind whistling through the trees—

"Confucius say, there are many kinds of food. There is food for the body; food for the mind; food for the emotions, and food for the soul. Man cannot live without food. Food is love, and man needs love to live."

"What have I got here, a Chinese fortune cookie?" Jordan thought to himself; but he never responded. He finished his soup and started on his plate of assorted salads.

The Oriental man got up and walked lightly to the buffet table and returned with a plate of selected greens. He ate slowly, meditatively; but his eyes kept looking up at Jordan, who was becoming very nervous of him staring.

"Do you mind?" Jordan said, giving him a look.

"Confucius say, food is love," the Oriental man said, his eyes twinkling like sparkling diamonds. "Man must have food to survive. If food is love as Confucius say, then man must have love to survive; *n'est ce pas?"*

"Who is this chink speaking French?" Jordan thought, annoyed with the interruptions. "Do you mind?" he said again.

"Patience," said the Oriental man. "All will become clear."

"What?" Jordan said, with a puzzled glare.

"Love, food, and the Gnostic Way," said the Oriental.

"*Oh no,*" said Jordan, under his breath. He shut his eyes for a moment and then opened them to see if the strange man was still there. He was. Jordan saw a golden light around the man's head, and the man gave him the most mystic smile he had ever seen and love poured out of his slanted eyes in a golden beam that shot straight to Jordan's heart like an arrow, and he instantly felt his appetite for the cornucopia of food completely and utterly sated and he had no more hunger for his eagerly anticipated Chinese dinner, and he stared in bewilderment.

All day long Jordan dreamt of the crab legs and assorted plates—roast beef, chicken wings, and his favorite, barbecued ribs—but he had no more appetite for any food, like he had just eaten a seven-course meal and could not possibly eat another morsel; and he just stared at the strange man smiling at him.

And then the Oriental man stood up and bowed respectfully and left the restaurant, seeming to glide out on a carpet of air. Jordan watched him leave, and as full as he was he had to have another beer to calm his nerves. He craved a cigarette, but that had to wait until he went outside, and the moment he stepped out the door he lit a cigarette and smoked three more by the time he got home feeling like he had been cheated of the dining pleasure of his Chinese dinner, and over and over he kept hearing the Oriental man repeating, "*Food is love, food is love, food is love...*"

When he got home he drank four more beer and a shot of rye to help him sleep, but the Oriental man came to him in his dreams and took him to the Dayaka Temple of Golden Wisdom in the city of Arhirit on the Etheric Plane. He was the guardian of the Holy Book of Gnostic Wisdom that rested on a lectern under a golden ball of light that sat on the spire of a hundred-story temple. The ball of light was so bright that its brilliance was greater than a hundred suns, and its rays reached out to the very edges of the Etheric Plane and spilled into the Mental Plane of Consciousness, the last of the lower worlds before the Soul Plane of God.

Jordan stood in front of the Holy Book of Gnostic Wisdom, and the golden light poured into his wanting soul. It poured and poured like he had been wanting the light forever, and when he could take no more he had to turn away.

"Soul also needs food, Jordan," said the Oriental man. "Confucius say, to get love you must give love. It is the law."

Jordan was speechless. He stared at the man with the braided ponytail and pointed beard who smiled and spoke again like the wind whispering through the trees: "Confucius say, man who eats more food than he pays for upsets the balance of the buffet table. The Gnostic Way is very hard, Jordan..."

23. Back to Square One

All day Saturday as he did his chores—going to the Laundromat after breakfast, grocery shopping on his way home, housecleaning and weekly bookwork—Jordan pondered his dilemma.

Elmer had assured him that his strange experiences weren't alcohol related, but he offered no other explanation for what he was going through other than that he was ready for the endgame; but every cell in his body screamed to be left alone.

"I don't need this in my life," he said to himself, afraid to speak out loud for fear of what might happen; but that didn't matter, because he heard Elmer's voice in his mind: "This is what you need in your life, Jordan. If left up to you, you'd never resolve the conflict in your heart. You need help, and I am here to help you."

Jordan was in the kitchen having a ham and cheese sandwich with a cold beer. He was too tired to be shocked and never bothered to reply; and he didn't even bother to light a cigarette with his second beer knowing that Elmer wouldn't approve. He was too tired to resist, and he sat in his chair beaten by what he could not fathom. It was so quiet in the kitchen that he heard his kitchen clock ticking.

He pushed his chair back from the table and stretched his legs and shut his eyes and just listened. It was like the ticking of his heart: tick, tick, tick. He began to doze off, and before he knew it he was standing outside his body looking at himself.

This was the third time he had seen his own body from outside his body, and he didn't know what to make of it. He should have been shocked, but he wasn't. He had no more fight in him, and he just went with his new mind-numbing experience. His head was slumped into his chest, and he was breathing heavily; but he was as alive and conscious as he could be in his other body outside his body.

"Now what?" he said, in hopeless resignation.

"Now you know that you are not your body," replied Elmer, who manifested out of thin air wearing a little black Greek fisherman's cap.

Jordan wasn't shocked by Elmer's appearance. Somehow he expected him to show up. He looked into Elmer's eyes, and said. "I give up. What do you want me to do? I'll do anything to make sense of my life."

"There's no turning back once you put your hand to the plow," Elmer said, with a glint in his clear blue eyes. "You have done so before, Jordan; and look where it got you, right back to square one. This is man's dilemma. He refuses to bear the fruit of his divine nature and keeps repeating his life over again; but your mind has been tilled once more, and the golden seed has sprouted with your surrender. You are ready to unshackle yourself from the chains of your mind and forge your own path out of the cave of spiritual ignorance and complacency."

"Forge my own path?" Jordan said, with awakened curiosity.

"I can show you the way out, but you must forge your own path to your true self. This is the paradox of the Gnostic Way. Did not Confucius say, you can lead a horse to water but you cannot make it drink? It is your choice, Jordan. Do you wish to drink the waters of Gnostic wisdom and resolve the conflict in your heart, or do you wish to continue suffering? It's entirely up to you."

Jordan stared at the big frame of his two hundred pound body stretched out and sleeping like a man who was thoroughly exhausted from struggling with himself, and then he looked at Elmer in his playful fisherman's cap staring at him with the most loving twinkle in his blue eyes, and said, "Do I have a choice?"

"Of course you have a choice. Soul always has a choice, Jordan; but you keep choosing to come back to square one. Haven't I got this through your thick head yet? There's no getting around it, my friend; you will just keep coming back to square one until you get life right. *Capisce?*"

"Not quite," Jordan calmly replied, much to his surprise.

"How can I make it any clearer? Your body there is not you. You use that body to have the experiences in life that you need to grow in your spiritual nature. This is the purpose of life. Soul must grow in life to realize its divine nature. That body is your vehicle, and when it has served its purpose it will be discarded like a used car and you will take on another body to continue your journey to your true self. Your problem is that you have come to the end of your journey as every soul must, because nature cannot evolve man enough to bear the fruit of his divine nature. Man must take evolution into his own hands to realize his true self, but he cannot do so alone; this is why I am here to help you complete your journey. *Capisce,* now?"

"Why do you use that word? It bothers me," Jordan said, unable to control himself. "I hate that word. It makes me feel stupid!"

"There is stupid and there is stupid," Elmer replied, without apology. "You are stupid in a non-stupid way, Jordan. This has been your problem your whole life."

"I have no idea what you're talking about," Jordan said, with anger in his voice; Elmer had stirred up his animus for his ex brother-in-law Peter Augustino.

Elmer smiled at Jordan's change of temperament. "Like I said, soul has two selves; one human, and one spiritual. The more soul is centered in the consciousness of its human self, the more spiritually stupid man is, despite the brilliance of his mind or conviction of his faith. This is why I have to break up the crusty soil of man's conceit that keeps the golden seed from sprouting. Man cannot do this alone. He needs God's help, and I am here to show you the way—"

Jordan suddenly swooshed back into his body and jerked himself awake. He looked for Elmer, but he was gone. He sat for a moment and then quickly jumped to his feet and drove straight over to Elmer's house.

"Elmer answered the door, still wearing his little Greek fisherman's cap. "Did I forget something?" he said.

"Yes," Jordan stammered.

"What did I forget?" Elmer asked.

"How do I forge my own path," Jordan asked, with some astonishment.

"Oh! I guess I did," Elmer said, and chuckled. "Well; let's get to it, then," he said, and took a Toonie out of his pocket and tossed the coin into the air and said, "heads you may come in, tails you may not."

It was heads, and Elmer invited Jordan into the house. Jordan sat at the kitchen table and Elmer went to the stove to stir his pot and put his burner on low; he was making pasta sauce with homemade Italian meatballs.

"Would you like to stay for dinner?" he asked.

"Why not?" Jordan said, feeling hungry from his busy day, and also because the aroma brought to mind Maria's spaghetti and homemade meatball sauce that was handed down from her mother. "But can we clear the air first?" he said. "I have to get something straight."

"What?" Elmer asked.

Jordan felt stupid for asking, but he had to make sure he understood what Elmer meant. "You said I have to get life right. What does that mean?"

"It means that you have to have the right kind of personality to forge your own path through life. You're too self-centered, Jordan. You have to break your ego-personality down and rebuild it on a new foundation," Elmer bluntly answered.

The aroma of the meatball sauce brought Jordan back to his wife Maria and his children. "Rebuild it? What does that mean?" he asked, with an ache in his heart.

"It means exactly what it means," Elmer replied, in an impersonal tone of voice like a professor giving a lecture. "Your ego-personality was formed without your consent, because this is the way karma works; but your ego-personality is much too small to contain your growing spiritual self. This is the root cause of all of man's personal and social problems. When the spiritual self hits the wall of its ego and is not allowed to grow in its divine nature, conflicts ensue. The cure to this problem is not more selfish indulgence at the buffet table of life, but the virtue of self-discipline. Man creates his own demons through selfish indulgence, Jordan; and the only way to complete your journey to your true self is to free yourself from the demons of your ego-personality. You have to die to the person you think you are and create a new personality free of your selfish demons. Didn't Jesus say, to find your life you must die to your life? And didn't St. Paul also say that even Satan is transformed into an angel of light? Well, Jordan; here you are, right back to square one. It's time to face the music and become the man you want to be."

"How, by dying to myself?" Jordan said, dazed by what he heard.

"Dying is too strong a word for you. You have to transform yourself. There is no other way to break the hold that your ego-personality has over you."

"Are you saying that my ego is my problem? That I have to transform my personality to get my life in order?" Jordan asked, with a painful grimace.

"Yes. And I will help you," Elmer said, and took the Toonie out of his pocket and tossed it across the table to Jordan.

Jordan caught it. "What do I do with this?"

"Why do you suppose I tossed that coin at the door?"

"You wanted to know if you should invite me in or not."

"Exactly. I let go and let God decide if you were ready to play the endgame. The Toonie landed heads, and I was given permission to let you into the mysteries of the Gnostic Way. Did you know that Julius Caesar is credited with the habit of tossing a coin to make decisions? His head was on the back of every Roman coin, so 'heads' determined the winner of each toss. Queen Elizabeth's head is on one side of that Toonie, and it landed heads when I asked God what to do. That coin you have in your hand represents both sides of your life, and it is the key to your freedom."

"How?" Jordan asked, completely mesmerized by Elmer's explanation.

"Don't take this lightly, Jordan. And don't let God decide every decision that you make. There is much more to this than meets the eye. This is a special key that opens the secret door to what Jesus called the kingdom of heaven, and I have given this key to very few people; but it's the best one suited to your nature. Whenever you have a decision to make that you cannot reason out on your own, toss your coin and let God decide for you. Heads you do, tails you don't. Let go and let God, as the saying goes; but you must trust the toss. If you are not true to the toss, you may as well throw in the towel and forfeit the game."

"Is this the endgame?" Jordan asked, completely forgetting that he did not even believe in God. "Tell me exactly what you mean by endgame?" he asked, looking directly into Elmer's eyes; but Elmer's clear blue eyes lit up with a light so bright that Jordan had to turn his face away, and Elmer got up and put his package of spaghetti into the pot of boiling water and sat back down again.

"The endgame is the final game of life," he explained, his eyes so bright that Jordan had to avert them. "St. Paul called the endgame putting away the old man and taking on the new creature. St. Paul's brought the Gnostic Way into the open, but his teaching has been misunderstood. By letting go and letting God with the toss of the coin you will initiate yourself into the secret teachings of the Gnostic Way. With every toss you forfeit your will to God and forge your own path through life; so don't make your decisions lightly. Your heart will tell you when to toss the coin; but never toss it unless you mean to live by the toss. That's your endgame, my friend."

Jordan was sober now; more sober than he had ever been in his entire life, like he had just been stunned awake by some kind of zap gun. "For what purpose?" he stammered. "What do I get by tossing this Toonie?"

Elmer laughed. "You are a creature of habit, aren't you? Well, your selfish creature has to be transformed into a new man for you to work your way out of Plato's cave of shadows and reflections. What do you get out of it? Freedom. You have to forfeit your will to God to realize your own will; that's the paradox of the endgame. But that's what you've always wanted, wasn't it? Well, now you have it in your power to become your own man; so let the game begin—"

A sudden blast of cold air rushed into the room and a chill shot through Jordan's body. Elmer's countenance changed, and his eyes were dark and suspicious. He got up and prepared his pasta dinner. "I'm taking two bucks off my next bill for this," he said, when he handed Jordan a plateful of spaghetti and meatballs. "That's not a bad deal for a Toonie, eh?"

"No," Jordan stammered, unsure of Elmer's behavior.

"You want a slice of bread with that?" Elmer asked.

"Yes, please," Jordan said, like a child at his father's table, and Elmer took the fresh loaf of Italian round bread that he had made earlier out of his pantry and placed it on a cutting board with a knife and placed it on the table.

"So how's business?" he asked, deftly twisting spaghetti onto his fork like Maria's family used to do. Jordan didn't know what to say. He waited a moment or two, and then replied, "Not bad."

"You still teaching?"

"Yes."

"Good. Hang on to that job. That's your gravy train."

Jordan was befuddled. He knew cranky Elmer was back, but he didn't know how to take him, so he ate his spaghetti in anxious silence, which wasn't hard to do because cranky Elmer hated small talk.

"You want some more?" he snapped at Jordan.

"No, I'm fine," Jordan responded, suddenly anxious to leave as he often did at his father's table when his father was in a bad mood. He wiped the remaining sauce from his plate with his bread and stood up. "Thank you, Elmer. I'll see you Thursday morning when I do your yard."

"Don't forget what we talked about."

"What?" Jordan asked.

"Are you dumb or what?" Elmer said, with a scowl on his wrinkled face.

When Jordan got into his truck he saw a mischievous twinkle in Elmer's eyes as he stood in the doorway, and as he drove away it occurred to him that he had put on that whole show just to teach him a lesson about his own personality.

24. Breaking the Pattern

Jordan drank several beer to think things through, and taking the last drag on his cigarette he reached into his pocket for the Toonie and stared at the coin for the longest time. "What have I gotten myself into?" he said. *"This is crazy!"*

He tossed the Toonie onto the counter by the phone, and as if on cue the phone rang and startled him. Jordan answered the phone on the fourth ring. It was a man from Toronto up for the week. "I've got a house here in the Beach and need someone to do my lawn," he said.

"I'm your man," Jordan replied.

"What are your rates?" asked the man, rather curtly.

"I have to see your yard first," Jordan replied, but the man insisted on a quote over the phone. "You can give me an idea, can't you?"

Jordan had dealt with Torontonians and their summer homes, and they could be aggressive and demanding, and he knew what he would be getting into; but he was a potential customer and gave him his standard rates.

"That's too much. I can get the same work for half the price."

"Then get it," Jordan said, and hung up the phone.

Jordan lit a cigarette to calm his nerves, but the phone rang again and startled him once more. "Look, I didn't mean to tick you off. Can't we make a deal?"

"What is it with you Torontonians?" Jordan snapped, taking his frustrations out on his aggressive caller. "Those are my rates, and they may be higher if there's more work involved. I have to see your yard first."

Jordan was staring at the Toonie as he spoke, and he got the strongest urge to toss the coin to decide what to do, and the man interrupted his thoughts: "You said you have a standard rate?"

"I do, but I can't stick by it. It depends on the job," Jordan said, and picked up the Toonie and tossed it into the air: *"Heads I do, tails I don't."*

The coin landed heads, and he took the job for his standard rate of forty dollars; but he regretted taking it because when he mowed the man's lawn he complained. "I'm not happy with the work," he said, "and I'm not paying."

"What's wrong with my work?" Jordan asked.

"Can't you see? The grass is too long. At this rate I'll have to have it cut every week. I'm not satisfied. You have to cut it shorter."

Jordan reached into his pocket and took out his Toonie. He tossed it into the air and said, "Heads I do, tails I don't." It was tails. "Sorry," he said. "You owe me forty bucks. Pay up or I'll take you to small claims court."

"That's what you'll have to do, then," said the Torontonian in an arrogant huff; and whether it was Jordan's imagination or not, he swore the man's face morphed into cranky Elmer's, and it startled him.

"Let's be reasonable," he said, coming to his senses. "Look, I give all my new customers a fifteen percent discount for the first three cuts. How does that sound?"

Jordan got paid and won over the arrogant Torontonian, but he wouldn't have had to go through that hassle had he not tossed the Toonie, and he wondered why God had put him through the experience; and after much reflection he thought the whole thing was too crazy to continue, and when his day's work was done he drove over to Elmer's house to return the Toonie.

Elmer answered the door wearing a Tilley hat and smiling, and Jordan saw that his eyes weren't dark and suspicious. "I've got your Toonie, Elmer. I'm not playing this game," he said, and handed him the coin.

But Elmer wouldn't take it. "Come in, Jordan," he said, and opened the door for him to enter. "Come in, come in. I think we should talk about your ego, don't you?"

"My ego?" Jordan said, taken by surprise; but he hesitated to step inside because he knew he would be swept away into that strange world of Gnostic Masters where the laws of physics didn't apply. "Here," he said, thrusting his hand out. "It's your Toonie. I don't want it."

"Did you toss it?" Elmer asked.

"Twice," Jordan said.

"And?"

"And what? The Toonie decided that I take a job that put me in a tricky situation with my new customer."

"Let's talk inside," Elmer said, and stepped aside for Jordan.

Jordan stepped into the house but didn't want to sit down. Elmer sat at the kitchen table and looked up at Jordan standing by the door. "Why do you think God wanted you to have the experience with that man with attitude?"

"I don't think God had anything to do with it," Jordan said, standing firm on his decision. "How can you make a connection with God and this Toonie? How can you be so sure God decides which way to go? It's all random chance, and I was a fool to fall for this crazy game. Here, take your Toonie back," he said, and placed the coin on the kitchen table.

Elmer glanced at the Toonie and then fixed his gaze on Jordan's eyes. "Why do you think the man with attitude refused to pay?"

"He said he wasn't happy with my work," Jordan said.

"Was your work any different from your other jobs?"

"No. I always cut my lawns the same length, unless I'm told otherwise. It's the best length for lawns in this part of the province. It looks nice and freshly cut and won't burn in scorching weather."

"Are you saying he wanted something for nothing?"

"I guess so," Jordan said, curious about Elmer's questions.

"You must have rubbed him the wrong way, Jordan. He was just trying to get back what you took from him, that's all," Elmer said.

"I might have ticked him off, but I didn't take anything from him. I worked for my forty bucks and he had to pay me."

"He wanted to make a point," Elmer said.

"What point?" Jordan asked.

"That he couldn't be pushed around."

"I don't like to be pushed around either. I did the work, and he owed me. What's fair is fair," Jordan replied, feeling justified.

"True. What's good for the goose is good for the gander," Elmer responded. "And what did you learn from this experience?"

"Nothing I didn't already know."

"And what is that?"

"That some people are assholes," Jordan said, and snickered.

Elmer gave Jordan a funny look, and said, "Ego is all about power, Jordan. That's how ego feeds the personality for the soul to grow; but how one gets his power is what the game of life is all about. Let me fill you in on the big secret of the Gnostic Way. The further one walks down this path, the more he will grant others their own freedom, and he will interfere less and less in another person's state of consciousness. This is axiomatic. And the more you play the endgame, the more conscious you will become of how the game of life is played; and you have to play by the rules or you will be dragged down to the same level that you were before you started playing the endgame. You don't want to go back to square one again, do you?"

"And what's wrong with that?" Jordan challenged.

"Have you seen the movie Groundhog Day?"

"As a matter of fact, I have. Why?"

"You're Phil Connors, Jordan," Elmer said, referring to the self-centered weatherman played by Bill Murray who was trapped in a loop of time that repeated the same Groundhog Day over and over again, and then Elmer picked up the Toonie and opened the door for Jordan. He put the Toonie into Jordan's pocket. "Trust me, you're going to need it," he said. "You can use your own coin if you want to, but this one has already been blessed. I'll see you at exactly the same time tomorrow."

"No you won't," Jordan said, but the following day his life repeated itself and Jordan found himself standing in Elmer's kitchen saying the very same thing; and the next day the same thing happened again; and the following day also, just like Phil Connors trapped in a loop of time in Groundhog Day.

Jordan was terrified to wake up each morning, knowing that he was going to repeat his day, and he tried to stay awake as long as he could to break the recurring pattern of his day; but however long he stayed awake, he found himself repeating the same day with his huffy customer and returning Elmer's Toonie, and it began to drive him crazy because he could not break the pattern of his same annoying day.

For seven straight days he experienced himself hopelessly repeating the same day over and over again, and he couldn't do anything to stop himself; but on the eighth day as he was about to leave his house to return Elmer's Toonie he felt the strongest urge to toss the coin and say, *"heads I do, tails I don't."*

It was tails and Jordan didn't return the Toonie, and his life returned to normal, or as normal as his life could be; but it didn't dawn upon him until later that by letting go and letting God he could also break the pattern of his normal life which was trapped in a larger loop of time, and he knew he had to play the endgame because there was no other way out of the life he had grown so tired of living.

25. A Gnostic Day

Jordan's life was back to normal, but it was different now; he knew something that he never knew before, and this changed the way he saw the world. *But he didn't really know what it was he knew!*

It was like he had an inner knowing that gave his life a meaning he never had before. He just *knew* that his life had purpose, and even if he didn't know what this purpose was it gave him hope.

When he thought about it, he never really knew if he ever had hope because hope wasn't in his lexicon of life experience. "Hope prolongs the agony of life," his father told him when he was ten years old. "It's a pauper's courage," and Jordan echoed his father's philosophy and got whatever he could however he could from life because that's all there was for him.

It was a no pie-in-the-sky philosophy, and his father molded and shaped Jordan's young personality; but it was too constricted for him to realize his divine nature, and the more he thought about his recurring day that kept him trapped in a loop of time the more he realized that life was a never-ending cycle of more of the same. *"That's it,"* he sighed, as he saw through the veil of space and time; *"that's Plato's cave—"*

He had no explanation for how he knew, but it didn't matter. It would have mattered before he met Elmer Coventry, but now he could see the light at the end of the tunnel; and he embraced the endgame with a passion that took him by surprise, like he had just awakened to life's divine purpose.

For three days he went to his jobs with this new sense of wonder, and on the fourth day he was going to supply for a class at Hampton High when he got the strongest urge to toss his Toonie and let God decide if he should have another cigarette before stepping into the school, and he froze in absolute terror.

"What if the toss says no?" he said to himself, with a paralyzing sense of fear of losing all the pleasure he got from smoking; and as compelling as the urge was to let go and let God decide what he should do, he could not toss the Toonie. He smoked another cigarette and went into the school.

But it bothered him all day long, and every time he lit a cigarette he felt a terrible sense of guilt, like he was committing a crime against himself. But still he could not abandon to the toss for fear of God saying no, and he continued to live his life with the guilt of smoking until Elmer put him wise.

"You have to build a history of making Gnostic decisions," said the man who had turned his world upside down, after Jordan mowed his lawn. They were sitting in the shade of the red maple in Elmer's back yard. Wearing his tan Tilley hat—he also had a green and brown one; plus dozens of various other hats that he wore for different occasions—and he looked comfortable and relaxed as he sipped his iced tea. "One small decision at a time, Jordan; that's how you build your trust in God."

As strange as it sounded, Jordan felt he knew what Elmer meant; but just to make sure, he said: "I have to make small decisions with my toss to build up my courage for the big decisions; is that what you're saying?"

"Yes. The toss is your narrow gate into the kingdom of heaven, and you don't want to frighten yourself off; do you?" Elmer said, and smiled.

Jordan looked at Elmer in his floppy Tilley hat with his warm smile and bright twinkle in his eyes, and for the first time since he had met the man he saw him for who he really was—*the Wayshower!*

"What am I to you?" Jordan asked, with the innocence of a child.

"You are to me what a petal is to a rose," said the Gnostic Master.

"That's too mystical," Jordan replied, snapping out of his child-like wonder. "Could you be a little more down to earth?"

Elmer laughed. "Life is full of symbols, Jordan; and when you learn the language of life you will see them everywhere. You won't be able to go across the street without knowing what's going to happen in China."

"Pardon me? What's crossing the street have to do with China?"

"That's the mystery, isn't it? Is life a random walk, or is it choreographed from above? Toss your coin, Jordan; and learn the truth of life."

It puzzled Jordan when Elmer spoke in riddles. "I have a couple of questions," he said, finding the courage to look a little deeper into the Gnostic Way. "Is life choreographed, as you say? And do we have free will or not? Because if life is choreographed we don't have free will, do we?"

"Of course man has free will," Elmer replied. "You're free to toss your coin and let go and let God, aren't you?"

"Yes, I am," Jordan said, feeling courageous. "But if life is choreographed, then the toss will come out as it's expected; won't it?"

Elmer slapped his thigh. *"That's the mystery!"*

"What mystery? That's fatalism, isn't it?" Jordan said, confused.

"Yes and no. That's the mystery of the kingdom of heaven. Did not Jesus say 'I am the way, the truth, and the life?' Jesus introduced the world to the Gnostic Way that leads to eternal life, but he was misunderstood by the world. The way of Gnosis is everywhere, and any experience man has can be an entry point into the kingdom of heaven; it all depends upon the individual. Like Christ's Parable of the Good Samaritan, man is free to make the choices he makes; but where do these choices take you? To eternal life or more of the same? The difference between deciding for yourself and letting God decide for you is the difference between a random universe locked in space and time and a divinely ordered universe of synchronistic wonder. When you decide for yourself you can never be sure of the outcome, and your life is a random walk through space and time; but if you let God decide for you, you can rest assured that you are in tune with the cosmic symphony of life and on your way home to the Soul Plane of God where all is one and one is all in joyful harmony. That's the point of the endgame, Jordan; to free yourself from the random walk of life."

Jordan was stunned. He didn't think there was an explanation for letting go and letting God, but Elmer made sense. "So if I don't let go and let God I stay trapped in a random universe where I can never be certain of the outcome; but if I let go and let God, then God will free me from the chaos of this random universe?"

"Yes," Elmer said, grinning like a proud father.

But Jordan grimaced. "Won't I be just a puppet, then? If I forfeit my freedom of choice to God, won't I just be a puppet for God? What happens to my free will when I let go and let God? Don't I lose it?"

"On the contrary, you will find it," Elmer explained, in his professorial tone of voice that Jordan found convincing. "That's the paradox of the final game of life. To find your life you must lose your life. That's the riddle of God, Jordan. And now that you have set your hand to the plow, plant all the golden seeds you can by letting go and letting God so you can grow strong enough to make your big decisions. Start small and build up to your big decisions. They won't go away, I promise you. They will hound you till the day you die, but the object of the endgame is to resolve the opposing factors of your decisions; so toss your way through your day and study your behavior. You will be surprised at what God will do for you."

It was threatening rain and Jordan had more lawns to cut. "I have to get back to work, but you've given me plenty to think about."

"Just remember, when in doubt about what to do, just ask for my help. I am always with you, Jordan," Elmer said, with the warmest smile.

"You are, aren't you?" Jordan said, feeling resigned to the strange relationship that he had with Elmer; and he gave him his hand to bid him a good day.

Elmer stood up and warmly shook Jordan's hand. "I'll see you when I see you, then. Have a Gnostic day, Jordan..."

26. The Mystic Carpenter Framer John

Peter Augustino always had trust, but he didn't know if it was God he trusted or some kind of higher power; he just trusted that everything would work out for him no matter what, and he never feared quitting a job when it was time to move on to a new experience and more life wisdom.

That's what Peter had to have more than anything else in his life, the wisdom that came with new experience—tree planting in northern Ontario, fruit picking out west, working with commercial fishermen, and construction work which he could always count on from his uncle Frank and in one of his family's pizzerias only when he had to, and in bookstores which he loved, and of all the sports that he enjoyed like cycling, skiing, and hiking he loved running most because he could run anywhere under any condition, which was always refreshing. New experiences gave Peter's life meaning, and he was forever on the move to satisfy his hunger for something new. Experience was food for his soul, but he always knew when he had exhausted the goodness of his experience and moved on to something different. He called the goodness of his experience virtue, which he learned from a mystic carpenter called Framer John, and one day years later Peter would make the connection of the virtue of honest work with the virtue of goodness in Plato's philosophy that Socrates deemed to be the noblest and which became Peter's favorite virtue.

From as far back as he could remember Peter felt trapped by life, like a prisoner in Plato's cave that he was to read about in Plato's *Republic*. He went to Mass with his family every Sunday morning, and he was even an altar boy for three years before he had to stop going to Sunday Mass when the symptoms of his strange ailment became too much for him to suffer but which only led the Italian community of Oakville to believe that he was possessed by the Devil that would not let him stay in church; but even after he left the Church he still felt trapped by life.

He never understood why he felt the way he did when he went to Sunday Mass, but the moment he stepped inside the church a sense of dread began to possess him and his chest slowly tightened and it was hard for him to breathe. Over time this feeling of terror grew worse and his breathing became more labored and constricted, and one Sunday morning while serving Mass for Father Dominic his breathing became so labored that Father Dominic was afraid he was going to choke and his mother and oldest brother Genaro had to rush him to the hospital; but after two days of testing they could find nothing wrong with him, and he was discharged.

He wasn't asthmatic, nor was he prone to panic attacks anywhere else; and everyone was thankful for his recovery, but the next time he served Sunday Mass he suffered the same symptoms and rushed out of the church and his breathing returned to normal an hour later. The doctor said he took his duties as an altar boy too seriously, and suggested he stopped serving Mass; but it wasn't serving Mass for Father Dominic that triggered his panic attacks, because for the next three Sundays he never served Mass and still suffered the same symptoms when he sat in the congregation with his family. That's when the widows all dressed in black started the rumor that the Devil possessed young Peter Augustino.

Peter stopped serving Mass, and he gradually pulled away from all church functions like baptisms, confirmations, weddings, and funerals; and he began to search for an answer to his feelings of smothering like he was being consumed by fire every time he stepped inside a church, regardless if it was Catholic, Protestant, Lutheran, Baptist, or whatever Christian denomination.

He never suffered panic attacks when he stepped inside a Mosque or Synagogue, which he tested out of curiosity; only when he stepped inside a Christian church, and he could not fathom why. And neither could anyone else, until one day while working on a new housing development in Oakville for his uncle Frank he made friends with a mystic carpenter who offered him a simple explanation when Peter shared with him his strange phobia after work one day—

"I think you have issues from a past life," he said to Peter, as they relaxed on the front steps of one of the houses they were working on. "You must be packing a lot of stuff to panic like that every time you step inside a Christian church. Have you ever thought of trying regression therapy?" Framer John, as he was called by everyone, asked Peter.

"Regression therapy? What's that?" Peter asked.

"Past-life regression therapy. Do you know anything about past lives, or what's called reincarnation?" asked Framer John.

"No, not really," Peter said.

Framer John revealed the ancient teachings of reincarnation and the radical new therapy of healing through past-life regression, and Peter honestly felt like he was sitting at the feet of some kind of mystic master. "That's what regression therapy is all about," Framer John explained, when they got back to Peter's problem. "The therapist will take you back to your former life that's responsible for your anxiety attacks, either by hypnosis or gentle talking; either way, my guess is that you had issues with your Christian faith in a past life. Maybe you were tortured and put to death for your beliefs. Who knows? But—" Framer John said, slapping his hand on Peter's shoulder and squeezing it with his powerful framer's fingers—"you must be discreet with whom you share this knowledge. It is much too powerful for the great unwashed. I would suggest you keep it to yourself for now, Peter."

This was all exciting new territory for Peter, but it felt strangely familiar; and he was willing to try anything to get to the bottom of his problem, so he decided to take the mystic carpenter's advice and explore past-life regression therapy.

Peter did some reading on reincarnation, and then one day serendipity brought him to a bookstore where he met a woman that had had past-life regressions from a therapist in London, Ontario who had trained at the C. G. Jung Institute in Zurich, and the woman recommend her highly. "She's very gifted, and not even forty years old," said the woman in the bookstore; and to Peter's amazement, Dr. Alexandra got to the root of his problem with only one session of regression therapy.

Peter learned that in a former life he belonged to a Gnostic sect of Christians called the Cathars, whose history could be traced to ancient times, and that he lived in the Languedoc region of France in the 13th Century when the Roman Church waged war against this heretic Christian sect and brutally slaughtered them all—blinding and dragging them behind horses and using them for target practice and burning many alive. "Kill them all; God will know his own," ordered the Cistercian Abbot Arnaud Amaury on the orders of his Pope, and the French army murdered all the Gnostic heretics in Languedoc including innocent Catholics and opened the door to the barbarity of the Spanish inquisition that was to follow.

The Cathars believed in the ancient teachings of karma and reincarnation and the blasphemous concept of two gods; a good creator god, and an adversarial god of evil, and the Cathars called themselves "good Christians." But they became a serious threat to the power of the Holy Roman Catholic Church because they did not need an intermediary for salvation, which made the Holy Church of Rome moot.

Peter was a *Parfait* who lived an ascetic life and enjoyed enormous spiritual freedom, and he was burned alive for his Gnostic beliefs when Pope Innocent 3rd called a formal crusade against the Cathars of Languedoc.

Peter was eighteen when he met Framer John on his uncle's site, and it was this mystic carpenter who introduced him to the ancient wisdom that ignited his quest for the Gnostic Way, and try as he may to locate Framer John after he had his one and only session with Dr. Alexandra, he would not see the mystic carpenter again until ten years later when he travelled to India. Every builder that Peter checked with said Framer John came and went as he pleased, and they didn't know any more about him. It was like he had vanished into thin air, and Peter never got to thank him for changing the course of his life, not even in India because he did not recognize that the man with the big walking stick was Framer John until it was too late.

The Sunday following his regression with Dr. Alexandra, Peter went to Mass and did not experience his dreaded panic attack; and neither did he experience it the following Sunday, nor the Sunday after, and he felt he was cured of his phobia of choking and smothering to death as he was in his past lifetime as *le Parfait* Simon Montpelier in Languedoc France in the 13th Century.

Nonetheless he knew in his heart that he did not belong in the Catholic Church, and he dropped his faith and became a seeker, starting with his research into the Gnostic teachings of the Cathars and other spiritual paths, with the strangest feeling that Framer John was guiding him in his quest.

Peter was working with one of his uncle's crews, who were building the forms for the cement foundations for new houses on a parcel of land that his uncle was developing in Oakville while Framer John worked on the houses that were ready to be framed, and Peter got to know him first when they met at the lunch truck that came to the site several times a day. Something about Framer John attracted Peter, and they had coffee and lunch together every day before Peter had to move to another site the following month; but before Peter left to work on his uncle's new site in Milton, Framer John introduced him to the mystical concept of "virtue."

"It's an elusive thing, Peter," Framer John shared with him that day, over a corned beef sandwich that he bought on site from the vendor while Peter ate his mother's crusty bun meatball sandwich; "but once you catch it, you won't be able to live without it. And when you have it, everyone wants to take it away from you."

Peter was mystified. "I don't understand. What do you mean by virtue?"

Framer John was not like any construction worker Peter had ever met. He didn't speak like the others, nor did he behave like them. He was polite and soft spoken, but not to be pushed around for his easy manners. He held his ground when he had to, but on the whole he minded his own business and gave everyone their space, and he could work with the best of them; but with one difference that singled him out from all the other workers: he refused to cut corners, even when he was ordered by his foreman to cut corners for the builder's bottom line.

"When you cut a corner in anything you do, you lose the virtue of your work and forfeit it to the great maw of life; and it will devour you whole if you let it," he counseled young Peter Augustino, like a benevolent father.

Peter listened without understanding, but he seemed to know what Framer John meant. His wisdom struck a chord with Peter, and he could not get enough of the strange man's company. Just being near him made him feel good, and one day he asked him why he felt that way whenever he was in his company—

"The more virtue a man possesses, the more attracted people are to him," explained Framer John. "It's like flowers and bees. Bees are attracted to flowers because they get their nourishment from the nectar, and man's soul needs virtue like bees need the sweet nectar of flowers; so naturally people that have a lot of life's sweet nectar will attract people like flowers attract bees. *Capisce*?"

Peter smiled at the word *capisce*, because John was not Italian. He didn't know what nationality he was, but being darker skinned and swarthier looking than most Europeans he thought he might be from the Middle East or India, especially with his neatly trimmed thick black beard; and there was such a knowing in his coal black eyes that Peter felt he was telling him something that he should know, and he pressed him on the sweet nectar of virtue—

"You've got me, John; I'm completely mystified. Can you tell me what you mean by your metaphor of the bees?" he asked, with bated breath.

"Try the Sufis. They've mastered the secret science of gathering honey," the mystic carpenter replied, and smiled again with that knowing smile that sent shivers up Peter's spine; but Peter had never heard of the Sufis, and he had to ask him what the Sufis were and what gathering honey had to do with anything—

"Sufism is a spiritual path. Check it out," Framer John answered, slapping Peter on the back as he stood up. "Go ahead, check it out—"

And the next morning Peter went straight to Framer John, who was standing by his pickup sipping on a coffee waiting to start his day. "I stayed up most of the night reading a book on Sufism by Idries Shah. Are you a Sufi, John?" Peter asked, all excited by his research on a spiritual path that was completely new to him.

"Nope. I'm on a different path," Framer John replied.

"I thought for sure you were a Sufi," Peter said.

"I'm not," he repeated.

"What path are you on, then?"

"The path of virtue."

"I don't understand," Peter said.

"You will once you catch the bug," Framer John said, with a look that pierced Peter's soul that let in the light of spiritual enlightenment.

"Bug?" Peter said, with a puzzled look.

"Virtue, Peter. Once the holy bug of virtue gets you, you won't be able to get enough of the sweet nectar of life; and you will drive yourself to distraction looking for a way to nourish the hunger in your soul. It will consume you. But you'll find your own path one day, Peter. You've got the right stuff."

"I do? How will I find my own path?" Peter asked, with wide-eyed wonder.

"It will find you when you are ready," Framer John replied.

"How can I make myself ready, then?" Peter eagerly asked.

"By not cutting corners," Framer John replied.

"You mean I shouldn't cheat?" Peter said.

Framer John's face lit up like the sun. "The beat poet Gary Snyder said it best in his poem 'Removing the Plate of the Pump on the Hydraulic System of the Backhoe,'" and the mystic carpenter quoted the short poem for Peter—

> Through mud, fouled nuts, black grime
> it opens, a gleam of spotless steel
> machined-fit-perfect
> swirl of intake and output
> relentless clarity
> at the heart
> of work.

Young Peter Augustino stared in awe at Framer John in his golden-brown Carhart carpenter's pants held up by his wide red suspenders and carpenter's belt and pouch with his big framing hammer and clean white T-shirt that he wore fresh to work every day, his muscular arms from swinging his framer's hammer with either hand that sunk a three and a half inch spiral spike into the studs with two swings, and his short, neatly trimmed black beard and Blue Jays cap, and he looked into his shiny coal black eyes and said, with surprising enthusiasm, like he had just been infused with a burst of intoxicating energy, *"Wow! What are you doing here? You should be teaching university somewhere!"*

"Life is my classroom," Framer John replied, with such a sweet smile that it warmed Peter's heart all day long; then he slapped Peter on the shoulder, and said, "Let's get back to work. We don't want to be late. An honest day's work for an honest day's pay; that's the relentless clarity at the heart of work and the secret to all the virtue that you will ever need. Talk to you later, Peter..."

27. A Desert Journey with Rumi's Teacher

Peter's past-life regression with the gifted Jungian therapist Dr. Alexandra changed his life. He knew little about reincarnation before his regression to his former life as Cathar Simon Montpelier in Languedoc; but after he experienced his own cruel death at the hands of the Church's Holy Army he had no desire to remain a Roman Catholic and went on a quest to reconnect with the Gnostic Way.

Framer John pointed him in the right direction, but it took time for Peter to realize the depths of the mystic carpenter's Gnostic wisdom. After he studied all he could find on the heretic Christian sect known as the Cathars, he followed up on what Framer John had told him about the "honey gatherers" and began to study the Sufi path and fell in love with the teaching stories of the Mullah Nasruddin.

He knew that Sufism was connected with what Framer John called "virtue," and that "virtue" had to do with not cheating, so it was logical to assume that "honey gathering" had to do with living life with honesty and integrity; but it proved to be more difficult than he expected, because everywhere he turned he saw guile, deception, downright gouging, and clever cheating—the kind of cheating that was just within the boundaries of the law, but morally reprehensible.

Peter discovered Rumi, whose words seemed to be impenetrable but which spoke the mystic wisdom of daily life; and the more he read Rumi's verse the more kinship he felt with the poet's intention, and he began to awaken to the mystic path that lay hidden in his every poem, starting with the shocking line from *The Tavern* that pierced Peter's heart: *"Why do you stay in prison when the door is so wide open?"*

The words screamed for his attention. For the first time in his life, Peter Augustino understood why he felt the way he did;

and the more he read Rumi's verse, the more he craved to escape from the prison of his own life. He found the key to his prison door in Rumi's poetry, and poem by poem he extracted a system to live by that began to free him from himself, just as Nasruddin taught with his story about the man who looked for the key to his house under the street lamp because the light was better there instead of looking for the key in his house where he had lost it. This was the essence of the Sufi path, which unlocked the door to Peter's heart.

"We seek from God the gift of courtesy," wrote Rumi, *"the grace of God is not for the discourteous,"* and Peter took this insight and added it to his arsenal of tools for spiritual survival in a world of liars, cheaters, and self-deceivers, training himself to be courteous with everyone regardless of their character. That's how he won God's grace and forged his path ferreting the secret teaching out of Rumi's poetry.

He took his cue from *A Children's Game*, one of Rumi's poems that spelled out the mystic path to one's true self; in a few lines he saw that to be free he had to adopt the attitude of a child and live like a man free of desire—*"All people of the planet are children, except the very few. No one is grown up except those free of desire."*

Peter adopted the mystic attitude of a desire-free life, which brought him to a Gurdjieff Group in San Francisco and a teaching called the Work that estranged him from his family and the world; but the harder he struggled to *non-identify* with his desires, the more honey he gathered to satisfy his spiritual hunger.

He could not understand how quickly he adapted to his quest for spiritual freedom as he lived Mr. G's teaching, as though he had lived this life before, which he had in his former life in Languedoc; so fighting off the desires of the flesh wasn't as big a sacrifice as it first seemed. But it was not enough to satisfy the longing in his soul, and with sadness in his heart he left the Group in search of something more.

The Work fueled Peter's hunger for new experience, and he went from job to job and interest to interest—long weekend cycling trips, hiking the Bruce Trail, canoeing in Algonquin Park, mountain climbing, skiing, and traveling to unfamiliar places, and reading, reading, reading—always searching for more "virtue" to satisfy the longing in his soul, which brought him to Konya during Ramadan where he met the keeper of Shams' tomb who took him to a Temple of Golden Wisdom in the inner worlds where he was blessed to read the Holy Book of Gnostic Wisdom that filled his heart with sacred knowledge and quenched his thirsty soul.

Peter learned that the keeper was Shams of Tabriz, the Gnostic Master who initiated Rumi into the secrets of the mystic path that changed the course of countless lives and continues to inspire seekers everywhere because Rumi's poetry is forever, but he did not know why he deserved the sacred privilege of reading the Holy Book and he asked the Gnostic Master, "Why me?"

"When the student is ready, the Master must appear," replied Shams, who came to Peter in a dream wearing his floppy hat at a funny angle and a wine colored robe and sandals. He looked comical and dignified at one and the same time, and Peter did not know whether to laugh or cry.

Shams looked into Peter's soulful eyes with a look that only a Gnostic Master can give, and in a voice rich as golden honey said, "Take your camel, Peter; and let us travel through the desert to the oasis of your heart. No Soul has ever reached the fulfillment of its quest, always journeying deeper into perfection and the Heart of God, and there is no room for despair in every step you take. Come, journey with me into the divine mystery of your true nature—"

Peter found himself on top of his camel with Shams in front on his own, and they journeyed through a desert of sand and howling wind. The biting sand stung his face and he had to cover it with the turban wrapped around his head, and as he drove his camel onward he had the strongest feeling that he had done this before, in a former life when he was a Bedouin merchant trading goods to support his family.

"Your name was Bahood," he heard Shams say, but Peter did not know if he heard Shams voice in his mind or carried by the wind. The storm grew fierce, and the sand bit through his garment and stung his skin and he instructed his camel to heel and got off and curled beside his camel until the storm blew over, as he had done many times before in his former life as the faithful Bedouin merchant Bahood.

When the storm abated he was covered in fine sand and alone with his faithful camel. Shams was nowhere to be seen, and he did not know if this was real or just a dream and didn't know what to do; but his Bedouin instincts took over and he got onto his camel and continued to his destination. "*Where?*" he woke up in a frightful state. "*Where is my destination?*"

28. The Crosscurrents of Life

Peter looked at his family members and invited guests as they drank and ate and danced and enjoyed themselves at his niece's lavish wedding reception, and he felt so out of place that he wanted to get up and walk away from his whole Italian heritage—his siblings and their spouses forever competing with new and larger homes and new and more lavish furniture just to be a notch above the others and firm their place in the hierarchy of social standing and another *Augustino Pizzeria* in another location to grow the family business and new cars and clothes and conspicuous jewelry, his uncles and aunts no different, and all of his nieces and nephews cut from the same acquisitive cloth and he said to himself, *"What am I doing here?"*

He took another sip of wine for his niece's sake, and with a sadness in his heart he confessed to himself, *"I don't belong here,"* but he knew he had to stay. He loved his niece dearly and wished the very best for her, so he pretended to enjoy himself to the very end of the reception; and when his niece was about to leave with her husband for their honeymoon in Cancun, she hugged her uncle and whispered into his ear, "Uncle Peter, I know how much you hate family gatherings; but I'm so glad you came. It means the world to me."

Of all his family members, his young niece whom he mentored because her alcoholic father was never there was the only one that Peter confided in, even more than his sister Maria, updating her along the way as if blazing a trail for her to follow, and when he found the key to the Gnostic Way eighteen years after her story-book wedding he sent her an email on his laptop from Italy to pass on to her the key to the secret way of life that he had spent most of his life seeking.

He dated his email to his niece, who was now forty with two teenage children, because he archived in a separate file everything that he wrote to her to keep a history of their special relationship; and this one was titled *"The Crosscurrents of Life,"* and dated *Sunday, June 13, 2010, Hotel Medici, Florence, Italy.*

His niece's name was Gioconda, after Peter's mother, whose origin meant "joy," and Peter affectionately called her "La Gioconda," the name of Leonardo da Vinci's mystic Mona Lisa; but everyone called her Gina except for her grandmother who on her deathbed refused to die until her namesake was by her side:

Ciao, cara. It's been a while since I've been in touch, but I'd like to share something with you that will connect all the pieces of the puzzle. I've been waiting a long time to share this with you, and this morning I was prompted by my Oracle to write you a letter; and you know that I always listen to my Oracle. (Oracle was Peter's word for the mysterious guiding principle of his life, which he borrowed from his favorite philosopher Socrates who always listened to his Oracle.)

I'm staying at the Hotel Medici in the historical center of Florence. I had to come to northern Italy after I read *Under the Tuscan Sun* by Frances Mayes, because I wanted to experience *la dolce vita* of the north after my fill of Reggio Calabria where I was born (did you know that John Milton used Calabria to describe the landscape of Hell in *Paradise Lost*?); but the more I explored this city so steeped in history, the more I realized why I have never identified with my native people.

I came to Italy to explore my roots, but my roots do not exist in my ancient Italian heritage, or even in my pubescent Canadian culture of hot dogs and Kraft Dinner. Sorry, dear; I'm just being my cheeky self. Anyway, that's what I discovered under the Tuscan sun, and I want to share my thoughts with you because I know how important it is for you to live your own life and be your own person.

Like me, you were born with a fire in your belly that no one else in our family seems to share (except your mother who married your father against the family's wishes and sacrificed everything for you and your brother), and you have realized your dream in the career you love and precious family. I know your marriage has been rocky, and that you wanted to walk away many times; but you stuck to your guns and made your dream come true, and I'm proud of how far you have come; but now that you're at the top of your game and your boy is off to university with your daughter soon to follow and you're settled into the home you dreamed one day of building, the fire in your belly has to find a new challenge or it will consume you.

If I may take an uncle's privilege and share with you another nugget that I mined in my quest for life's meaning, let me tell you quite frankly that our family demons keep us from being the person we are meant to be; and given our last talk about the animus that your brother stirs up in you, I suggest it's time for you to let go of your demons too because if you don't they will only consume you. This is why I had to come to Italy one more time. I had to put my family demons to rest once and for all so I don't have the baggage of our *family shadow* (unresolved family karma) for the rest of my journey back home; but where is home, you ask?

I've been on this journey for many years, but I never knew my destination until I found the path to my true self; and this is what I want to share with you this morning from my beautiful room in Hotel Medici. I want to spare you all the time and heartache that it took me to discover this simple truth, and you would do me proud to ponder what I have to share for the rest of your journey through life.

If I may then, beneath the surface of life flows a mystic river of eternal life that no one knows exists; and this river flows from the Great Ocean of Love and Mercy to create life in these lower worlds and then flows back to God again with the new souls that it has created. I can't prove that this other river exists of course, because one can only prove this for oneself; but I can tell you how to find it.

The Preacher tells us in *Ecclesiastes* that all the rivers run into the sea but the sea is never full and the rivers return to the place from where they came. This speaks to the River of Life, a symbolic reference to reincarnation; but the Preacher also speaks to the River of God that flows through life that no one sees.

The River of Life flows back into itself in a never-ending circle of life and death, and the River of God flows through life back to the Great Ocean of Love and Mercy where we came from. This is what the Preacher concealed in the *Book of Ecclesiastes,* and what I finally discovered for myself in my quest for life's meaning.

Everyone is trapped in the River of Life, destined to return to life over and over again by the imperative of their own karma; but after many lifetimes the soul of man becomes so tired of life that it wants to break the cycle of reincarnation.

I wanted out of life from an early age. That's why I felt like I never belonged in my family, or anywhere else for that matter. I went on a quest to find out why I felt this way, and I learned that I had simply outgrown this tiresome old world. I know it sounds like uncle Peter has lost it again, but I haven't; I've never been saner in my entire life. I just don't get out of life what other people do, because life could never satisfy the hunger in my soul to be all that I longed to be.

You have no idea how I hungered for life, Gina; that's why I could never settle down. I needed all the goodness that life could give me, and I tried everything that my inner guide inspired me to do; but it was never enough. That's why I became a seeker. I had to find a source of energy that would satisfy my longing to be whole, and I did not stop looking until I found the path that led to my true self.

When I drove you to university for your first year because your resentful bother refused to take you, you told me how important it was for you to be your own person, which you had to fight to become because our Italian heritage resisted you all the way; you weren't supposed to get a career and become the person you longed to be, because all good Italian girls were supposed to stay home and take care of their husband and family. Well, you're at the top of your game now Gina; but as you said to me at the airport restaurant before I left for Italy, "Where do I go from here?"

You have a million dollar home on the Niagara Escarpment that is the envy of our family, and a career that tops the salary of all your uncles and cousins, and a family that adores you; but you still long to be more, and you do not know where to turn. This is life's dilemma, and few people ever work their way out of this conundrum. But you don't have to go to India to study at the feet of some guru (I tried that), nor do you have to go to Mount Athos and beg the monks for a few pearls of precious wisdom (I did that too); all you have to do is shift your focus on life and you will have all the purpose that you need to give your life more meaning.

You see *cara mia,* as long as we're stuck in the River of Life we will always be fighting against the currents of this other river, which is pulling us to our eternal self. You find yourself exactly where I was all those years ago, trapped in the crosscurrents of these two rivers; and you don't know which way to go. But I can promise you that you don't have to go anywhere to free yourself from the crosscurrents of life. You can have your cake and eat it too if you are you willing to pay the price.

You know how hard you had to work to get to where you are today; but you have to work even harder to get to where you are being pulled to go. As long as we are stuck in the River of Life we are forever becoming who we are; but once we make the shift to the river of eternal life we cease becoming and just ARE, like the acorn seed that has finally become an oak tree. So, what is the secret to shifting our focus from the River of Life to this other river and be who we are meant to be?

Our personal identity defines who we are becoming, but the unique self that we have created through the natural process of karma and reincarnation cannot bear the fruit of our true nature, and we have to finish what nature cannot complete by crossing over into this other river and living our life with karmic awareness and responsibility; and herein lies our problem.

In Plato's *Republic*, Socrates tells us that man is like a prisoner in a cave who takes the shadows and reflections on the cave wall to be the reality of life; but the shadows and reflections are an illusion of the mind. Reality exists outside the cave, but we all need help to escape from the illusory world of shadows and reflections. No one can escape from the cave of life's illusions without help from someone who has already escaped, and that's what I was looking for all my life.

Many people know how to escape from the illusory reality of the mind, but they cannot escape because the sacrifice is too great; so just what price do we have to pay to become the person we are meant to be?

I felt trapped from an early age by my Roman Catholic faith (rumor has it that I'm still possessed by the Devil), and it took years before I sacrificed my faith for the wisdom of the other river. I had grown as much as nature could take me, and not until I shifted my focus to the other river could I satisfy my longing to be free; that's why I could never settle down, because the more life I experienced the more I satisfied my longing to be free. But still I felt trapped by life.

My shift to the other river began when I met a carpenter called Framer John on one of Uncle Frank's building sites after I graduated from high school, whom I met again ten years later when I went to India to see the Dalai Lama, and he introduced me to a teaching that helped me cross over to the other river. I took Framer John's words to heart and learned how to gather the sweet nectar of life from every new experience; and when I had acquired enough virtue I was pulled into the currents of the other river and satisfied the longing for my true self.

It's still a mystery to me how it all happened, but I know it has to do with this mysterious thing that Framer John called virtue. He told me when I worked for Uncle Frank all those years ago that this mysterious virtue cannot be taught but must be caught, and after many years of living my life in this other river I finally saw what he meant by virtue, and it is simply the essential energy of life. Western cultures call it Holy Spirit, and in the

Orient they call it Chi, but by whatever name we call the vital life force, it is the essence of our true nature; and not until we have acquired enough virtue will we become the person we are meant to be.

Socrates tells us how to cross over to the other river, and so does Jesus; but I assure you *cara mia*, it's not really that mysterious. This knowledge has always been kept secret because this is how it's meant to be, but once you grasp the principle of the secret way of life you will understand why it has to be this way.

If I may, then. As we grow from life to life in the endless cycle of life and death, we evolve in our own individuality; but life cannot satisfy our longing to be whole through natural evolution. We have to cross over to the other river and take evolution into our own hands to become the person we are meant to be; and we complete what nature cannot finish by learning how to catch this precious life force called virtue, and we do this by simply being a good person.

Of course, being a good person is not so simple; because the moment we cross over to the other river we go against the currents of life and threaten the status quo. They have a saying in jail that no good deed goes unpunished, and the same can be said of life because good people prick the conscience of everyone that does not want to make the moral effort to be good; which is why Jesus counseled us to do our good deeds in secret where the thieves and rust cannot get at our virtue.

It takes a lot of courage and wisdom to be a good person, because being good means the unselfish giving of yourself to others, and man is by his primal nature a selfish creature; so the more we strive to be good, the more resistance we will get from the world because too much virtue threatens the status quo.

Great spiritual leaders have always suffered at the hands of society because they had too much virtue. Socrates was condemned for corrupting the youth of Athens with his "seditious" philosophy; Jesus was crucified by the Romans for threatening their power with his teaching of love; and Mahatma

Gandhi threatened the British Empire's hold on India with the simple power of moral goodness. People of great virtue have always been maligned and murdered and sent to prison because they threatened the status quo; but that's just the way life seems to be.

The River of Life flows back into itself, and the other river (which Jesus called "water of eternal life") flows through life and back to the higher worlds of God; so the harder one tries to break free of the currents of daily life, the more resistance he will get from the status quo. This is why it's so hard to be your own person and why the secret way of life has always been kept hidden from the eyes of the profane.

Life fought you at every turn, Gina; because you wanted to break free of convention and pursue your own dream, which you did with a tenacity that was unforgiving; and now that you have been accepted for all of your accomplishments (despite the envy of family and friends), you still crave to satisfy your longing to be more; which is why I was prompted by my Oracle to write you this letter.

All the spiritual teachings of the world talk about sacrificing ego to be our true self, but this is a tragic misunderstanding of the dynamics of spiritual growth. Ego cannot be sacrificed, because ego is endemic to our identity; it has to be transformed by shifting our focus on life by simply being a good person.

My mentor Socrates spelled out this dynamic in very simple terms. Man must live a life of virtue to free himself from the illusory world of his own ego, because a life of virtue purifies the ego and satisfies our longing to be whole. *"And what is purification but the separation of the soul from the body, the habit of the soul gathering and collecting herself into herself,"* said Socrates in Plato's *Phaedo*; but ego resists all of our efforts to be purified. Why?

Because ego is insatiable and can never be satisfied. The consciousness of life is not pure enough to satisfy our longing to be whole, because the *enantiodromiac* consciousness of life is both positive and negative (sorry for the big word, but all *enantiodromia* means is that life is always in a state of change from one thing to another), and ego has to be true to its selfish nature and craves more and more life experience; this is why it's so hard to purify the consciousness of our ego self.

We need the pure consciousness of virtue to satisfy our longing to be whole; but to satisfy our longing we have to reverse the flow of our ego-driven life and start giving back to life instead of always taking. But it takes courage, skill, and great wisdom to resist the currents of the status quo. This is why being a good person is much easier said than done. So it all boils down to this, *bella mia*: do we want more of the same, or do we bite the bullet and start giving back to life?

Many years ago in the lake District of England where my favorite poet was born, I decided to bite the bullet and made a list of all the virtues that I would live by—kindness, forgiveness, compassion, courage, patience, and so on, putting goodness at the top of my list (my inspiration was "Character of the Happy Warrior," by William Wordsworth: "...*he labors good on good to fix, and owes to virtue every triumph that he knows*"), and I tried my best to be a good person by taking one virtue every morning and practicing it all day long; and, as that mystic carpenter Framer John said to me when I was so wet behind the ears but hungry for life wisdom, *"Be true to yourself and never cut corners in what you do,"* because cutting corners compromises our integrity and feeds the demons of our *shadow* self (the unconscious side of ego); and I can tell you *cara mia*, the most difficult part of my journey to my true self was learning how to master the impossible art of compromise!

This has been a long discourse, but I woke up this morning compelled by my Oracle to share my thoughts with you. I will be leaving Florence tomorrow. I may go to France next. I have a few more ghosts to put to rest in Languedoc...

Be good,
Uncle Peter

29. The Cottier Jeremy O'Conner

"Have a Gnostic day?" Jordan repeated, as he drove to his other jobs; and as he mowed his three lawns under the threat of rain with a few quick downpours now and then, he had to admit that he didn't really know what Elmer meant. He laughed at the irony of his predicament. *"How can I have a Gnostic day if I don't know what a Gnostic day is?"*

Since he met Elmer his world had been turned upside down, like he was living in a parallel universe where the laws of physics did not matter; but he was still bound to a universe of natural laws that he once believed was all there was, and he didn't know what was real and what was not anymore.

"But what can I do about it?" he asked himself, as he drank his second beer after his day's work. He lit another cigarette, feeling guilty for lighting up, and he took a long drag to spite his guilty feeling; and then he thought—*"What if I tossed the Toonie for another beer?"* And he felt a tingle of excitement at the challenge.

He took the Toonie out of his pocket and stared at it for the longest time trying to decide what to do, but the longer he stared the more he froze; and the Toonie began to glow with an eerie foggy iridescence.

The light grew bigger and more iridescent as he stared, and the more the light grew the more it encircled his body and pulled him back through time; and when the light enveloped his entire body he knew he was Jeremy O'Conner and lived in Ireland with his wife and family in the year 1846 when the potato famine was at its worst.

Jeremy was an indentured cottier who had to help bring in the annual harvest of wheat to pay rent on his windowless mud home that he was allowed to build on his landlord's estate who also let him farm a small plot of land to feed his family.

Like every cottier in Ireland, Jeremy O'Conner was desperately poor; and his son and daughter were dying of hunger when the potato blight swept throughout the land like a vengeful curse from God. His wife was pregnant with another child, and they had run out of food in the middle of the summer hunger, and he didn't know what to do. His potato crop was blighted, and he had nowhere to turn and the terrible thought came to him again but he prayed to God for strength and was spared for another day; but he no longer had the strength to ask God for help, and it did not matter if he went to hell for what he was about to do, and the last words that came out of Jeremey O'Conner's mouth were, "Lord Jesus, have mercy on my soul..."

The clunk of the Toonie as it hit the floor brought Jordan back to himself, but the guilt of what he had done weighed so heavily upon his soul that tears came gushing to his eyes, and he cried for hours before the memory began to fade and all that remained was the hollow in his soul for what he had done to his wife and family, and he thought of his wife Maria and Mark and Lisa. He downed another beer in two swallows and flopped his body onto the couch and fell into a dead sleep.

Elmer came to Jordan in his dreams and lifted him gently out of his body and brought him to a temple of healing in the inner worlds; and a woman in white with a radiant smile asked Jordan to have a seat in the middle of the room and close his eyes and listen to the sweetest music he had ever heard.

"Let the Sound of God flow through your body," said the women in a melodious voice, "and let all your sorrows wash away into the river of love... "

It was 2:45 A. M. when Jordan woke up. He was hungry and went into the kitchen and made a cold cut turkey sandwich and another one of ham, and he turned on the TV and dozed off watching a late movie.

He woke up at ten and lit a cigarette before making coffee, and then he washed up. He didn't bother to change clothes and went straight to work after he had his coffee and four pieces of toast and honey.

Jordan had five lawns to cut, but before he could do the last two it started to rain and he had to shut down. On the way home he decided to stop at the liquor store for a bottle of rye, but he was hit with the strongest desire to toss the Toonie to let God decide what he should do. He pulled into the parking lot and lit a cigarette to calm himself down, but he could not fight the urge to toss the Toonie.

If he was not true to the toss, he would have to forfeit the game and go back to square one. *"Square one?"* he said to himself, to his surprise. *"That's right back here, isn't it? This is square one. So what does it matter if I don't toss the Toonie?"* he asked again, trying not to sound like he wasn't desperate; but he was. He couldn't fight the urge to toss the coin, but he didn't want to forfeit his hard liquor in case God said no. *"What's the point of this again?"* he asked himself, as if he didn't know; but it was to choose the random universe of personal choice, or the universe of order where God chose for him. *"So the point of letting go and letting God is what, exactly?"*

"Again, I have to tell you," he heard Elmer's voice, in his distinct Kentucky drawl; but his body wasn't there. "The point is to free you from yourself," Elmer confirmed, with a sternness in his voice. "Now toss the Toonie and get on with it. You can't run away from square one. It's the beginning at the end of the line."

Like a bolt out of the blue Jordan realized that square one was the NOW of life and the gateway into the kingdom of heaven, and he held the key that unlocked the secrets of the Gnostic Way in his hand; and he knew that if he let God decide he would have a Gnostic day. He tossed the Toonie into the air without another thought, and before it landed in his hand he said, *"Heads I do, tails I don't—"*

Jordan could not believe his eyes. He thought for certain that God would say no, and he was so relieved that he flushed red with guilt for God's decision; but as guilty as he felt, he went into the liquor store and bought a forty ounce bottle of Canadian Club rye whiskey; and when he got home he had a double shot to calm his nerves. And then he lit a cigarette to think the whole thing through.

He stared at his bottle of rye as he dragged on his cigarette, wondering why the Toonie had landed heads when he was so convinced it was going to be tails, and the longer he thought about his toss the more he doubted the point of the endgame, because in his heart he knew that he should not have bought the bottle of rye and he was utterly puzzled by God's decision.

"I guess God doesn't mind if I drink whiskey," he said to himself, to assuage his foreboding sense of guilt; but no matter how much he tried to convince himself, he could not stem the feeling that he had betrayed himself like he had betrayed his wife and family, not once but twice; and he wanted to crawl into a hole and die.

30. Elmer's Southern Corn Bread

It was Saturday and not raining. Jordan had a leisurely breakfast and did some bookwork and then went out and mowed the lawns he never got to do Friday. His last lawn was two blocks from Elmer's house, so he dropped by on his way home.

Elmer was making Southern cornbread the way his stepmother used to make it, flavored with bacon grease and cooked in a cast iron skillet, which he loved straight out of the oven slathered with butter. "Come in, come in," he said, with a white apron around his waist and white chef's hat. "I'm making cornbread. Do you have any hobbies, Jordan?" he asked, as he wiped the table.

"Just golfing," he replied, smiling at Elmer's apparel.

"Can I offer you a cup of coffee?" Elmer asked, and turned on the faucet to rinse the cloth he used to wipe the table.

"Please," Jordan said, and sat in his usual chair.

Elmer poured Jordan a cup from the fresh pot he had just put on, as though he was expecting Jordan to drop by. "What's on your mind?" he asked, placing Jordan's green mug on the table. "I'll get you some milk—"

Jordan stirred his coffee. "I tossed the Toonie yesterday."

"Oh? And?" Elmer said, as if he didn't know.

Jordan checked Elmer's eyes before answering. "I let my Toonie decide for me yesterday. I didn't want to, but I got the strongest urge to toss it when I went to the liquor store. Tell me the truth, Elmer; did God nudge me to toss the Toonie?"

Jordan could not believe what he had just said, and he fell dead silent and recoiled into himself like a frightened child. Elmer gave Jordan a big smile, his round wrinkled face lighting up like a miniature sun. "Soul wanted you to toss the Toonie. Soul is who you are, Jordan. Soul is your true self, and your true self wants you to come back to God. By the way, what did you ask God to decide for you?"

"God or chance?" Jordan quickly responded, in his skeptical defense.

Elmer did not answer. Instead he got up and put the cast iron skillet with his cornbread batter into the oven and checked the temperature. "I have learned over the years that my corn bread comes out a littler nicer at a lower temperature," he explained. "It bakes more gently and comes out soft just the way I like it. So, what decision did you ask God to make for you?" he repeated.

Jordan didn't know why, because one part of him saw how absurd it was to believe that God had decided for him with his Toonie, but being in Elmer's presence affected him in a strange way. "I didn't know whether to buy a bottle of rye or not, so I tossed the Toonie; and the toss said yes, so it was okay for me to buy it."

"And how did you feel about God's decision?"

"Honestly?' Jordan asked.

"You wouldn't lie to me at this stage of the game, would you?"

"No, I don't think so," Jordan said, craving a cigarette. "I was happy that I could buy my rye, but it didn't sit right with me. I felt like—"

Jordan stopped in mid sentence. He really wanted a cigarette, but he couldn't light one up in Elmer's presence. He waited another moment. "I felt like I had betrayed myself. I don't know why, but that's how I felt."

"That was a momentous decision for you, wasn't it?"

"What, buying the bottle of rye?'

"Tossing the Toonie," Elmer corrected.

"Yes, it was," Jordan confessed.

"You really turned the heat on with that decision, didn't you? But now you're free to buy your booze anytime you want, aren't you?"

"I guess so," Jordan said, suddenly feeling nervous.

"God said it was okay, so it must be okay," Elmer repeated, in what sounded very much like old cranky Elmer's sarcastic voice.

Jordan was very suspicious now, and he saw the absurdity of God making up his mind for him with the Toonie; but he had to see it through. "If God said it was okay for me to buy my bottle of rye, then I guess it must be okay for me to drink whiskey; don't you think?"

"What I think is about as important as a fart in a windstorm. What matters is what you think. Do you think it's okay to drink whiskey?"

"I bought the bottle, didn't I?" Jordan replied sarcastically.

"Then why do you feel that you betrayed yourself?"

"I don't know. That's what I came to ask you, I guess."

"What is God, Jordan?" Elmer asked, looking Jordan in the eye.

"How in the hell would I know?" Jordan shot back, feeling like a fly about to be swatted.

"Do you still doubt the existence of God?" Elmer asked, with a smile that Jordan couldn't read but which irked his ire.

"I have no proof that God exists, do I?" he retorted.

"You have more proof than you realize," Elmer answered.

"Do you have proof that God exists?" Jordan challenged.

"I don't need proof; I know. To know that God exists you have to open your spiritual eye, which the Toonie helped you to do. Perhaps you bit off more than you can chew with your toss for the forty ouncer. Perhaps you should bake your bread at a lower temperature. But you've crossed that Rubicon now, haven't you?"

"What do you mean?" Jordan asked, suddenly feeling terrified.

Elmer looked into Jordan's frightened eyes, as if to prepare him for what was to come, and with the kindest look and warmest smile he gave it to Jordan right between the eyes: "God gave you permission to buy your whiskey. It's up to you now if you want to continue buying whiskey or not; but you can never revisit that decision with your Toonie."

A sudden weight descended upon Jordan's shoulders, and it sunk his spirits so low that he felt like crying, and in the same frightened voice that he spoke to his father with so many years ago he said, "I didn't want to toss the Toonie. I was afraid of the outcome, but I couldn't help myself. I had to know. I thought the Toonie would say no. I don't know what's going on, Elmer. I'm so confused—"

"You have to adjust to the light, Jordan," he heard Elmer say, in a much softer, compassionate voice. "It takes time to adjust to the light outside the cave of shadows and reflections. This is why most people turn back. The light is too bright for their eyes, and they rebuke it. With every step you take on the Gnostic Way, the more responsible you must be. You don't like what you see because it threatens who you think you are; that's why you feel guilty for buying your bottle of rye. Ponder this, Jordan; why do you feel guilty that God granted you permission to drink whiskey?"

"I don't know; I just do," Jordan said, fighting back his tears.

"Ponder some more," Elmer implored, somewhat sternly.

"Maybe it's because of what alcohol did to my father," Jordan replied, feeling a tide of emotions breaking through the wall of his mind.

"So why do you think God would grant you permission knowing what alcohol did to your father?" Elmer asked, as he got up to check his cornbread. "Do you think God wants you to become like your father?"

Fear seized Jordan. *"I hope not!"*

"Then why do you suppose God granted you permission to drink rye whiskey?" Elmer asked, sounding just like his father as he shut the oven door. He turned and looked at Jordan, and Jordan froze like he had just seen a ghost—

"What the hell's going on?" he exclaimed, and jumped to his feet and dashed out the door. Elmer made no effort to call him back.

31. Extending the Sacred Contract

When he got home from Elmer's house he drank half a dozen beer and three shots of rye whiskey and passed out. The phone woke him up.

"What the hell's keeping you?" Derrick asked.

"What? Who's this?" Jordan asked, groggy.

"Derrick. I've been waiting for half an hour. Are you coming?"

"Oh," Jordan said, rubbing his eyes. "Yeah, I'll be there shortly."

"Hurry up," Derrick said, and hung up.

Jordan showered and shaved and put on a pair of shorts and his favorite golfing shirt that Maria had given him one Christmas and drove to *Hampton Golf and Country Club*, picking up a large coffee at Tim Hortons on the way. Derrick was in the clubhouse waiting.

"About time. What did you do, tie one on last night?"

"Yeah," Jordan said, taking a look around. He recognized his bank manager and golfing partner and said hello. Turning to Derrick, he said, "What are we playing for today? Buck a hole?"

"Make it two bucks. Are you ready?"

"Give me a minute to finish my coffee. I'm not awake yet."

Jordan met Derrick in the staff room at Hampton High School. He was a math teacher and twice divorced. He had two children with his first wife and they were both in university. His second wife left him for another woman. Derrick spent most of his summers golfing and curling in the winter months, and like Jordan he liked his beer. They had a standing golf date every Sunday morning, and they always played for a buck a hole; but Jordan's heart wasn't in the game, and he lost six of the first nine holes. Derrick couldn't believe his luck, and rubbed it in—

"What do you say we double the stakes, Jordan?"

Jordan wasn't paying attention. "What?"

"Let's double the stakes?"

"Let's make it an even five."

"Sure, why not?" Derrick said, but Jordan couldn't concentrate like he used to. His mind was not there, and after the second round he paid Derrick what he owed and apologized for playing so poorly. Derrick wanted to go another round, but Jordan's heart just wasn't in it; and he sat in the clubhouse drinking a beer to reflect upon his feelings.

Not in a million years did he expect to feel the way he did, but as he stared out the windows of the clubhouse and watched the men and women in their colored shorts and shirts pulling their carts to their little white ball he saw the absurdity of it all and reached into his pocket for his Toonie and tossed it into the air—*"Heads I stop playing golf, tails I don't."*

He caught the Toonie in his right hand and slapped it onto his wrist and stared and stared and stared at his destined fate—

"Well, are you coming or not?" Derrick asked.

"No," Jordan replied, and put the Toonie back into his pocket. He thanked Derrick for the game and said, "I quit. No more golf, Derrick. I have better things to do with my life," and he drove straight to Elmer's house and knocked on his door and waited, and waited, and waited.

Elmer's car was in the driveway, and he felt that Elmer was home; but he wasn't answering the door. Jordan knocked again, much louder; and he waited some more; and then he saw Elmer walking up the driveway.

"Hello, Jordan," he said with a happy smile, and gave Jordan his hand to shake. Jordan felt a surge of energy shoot through his body, and it felt so good he didn't want to let go. Elmer clasped Jordan's hand with his other hand and said, "You've made another big decision, haven't you?"

"Yes," Jordan said, with tears in his eyes.

"That wasn't so hard, was it?" Elmer said, letting go of Jordan's hand.

"I don't believe I did it," Jordan said, the tears streaming down his cheeks; but he wasn't even aware that he was crying.

"Let's go inside and talk about it," Elmer said, and opened the door for Jordan to enter. Jordan sat at the kitchen table and Elmer took out the two colored mugs that he always used and filled them with the fresh coffee that he had brewed for the special occasion; but he didn't' have to tell Jordan that he was waiting for him to extend his Sacred Contract. In his heart, Jordan knew; and he looked into Elmer's eyes and couldn't stop himself from crying.

"I can't believe I did it," he said, sniffling like a child. "I loved golf so much that it cost me my first marriage. Did you know that?"

"It was a contributing factor," Elmer said, with a smile that lit up Jordan's heart. "That was the Sacred Contract you made with Maria, and you had no choice but to play it out. No one has. A Sacred Contract is a Sacred Contract, and Soul is obligated to see it through. But now here you are, ready for a fresh start. If you had your druthers, Jordan; would you go back to your wife Maria and your children?"

Jordan sniggered at the thought. "How?"

"Extend your Sacred Contract," Elmer replied.

"And how would I do that?" Jordan asked, not even knowing what Elmer meant by Sacred Contract; he was beyond trusting Elmer, he simply knew that whatever he told him would be true.

Elmer smiled again, his eyes so full of love that Jordan felt he was in heaven, and then Elmer went to one of his kitchen drawers and took out a file that was labelled Jordan and Maria and put it on the kitchen table. He opened the folder and took out the Sacred Contract that Jordan and Maria had signed on the other side and read the clause that extended their Sacred Contract indefinitely, and then he took out a pen from his shirt pocket, and said, "Sign on the dotted line."

Jordan took the pen from Elmer's hand and looked at the bottom line of his Sacred Contract with Maria and signed his name, and in an instant he was in Sharon's apartment deciding whether he should stay the night with her or go home to his children. Sharon coaxed him with another beer.

"You're perfectly welcome to stay," she repeated, hiding her desperation behind a false smile; but time stopped for Jordan. Between Sharon's invitation to stay the night and his fateful response, a scene flashed before his eyes of his life in Hampton Beach and all that had brought him there, and before he gave his answer he saw Elmer's face and loving smile. "Well?" Sharon asked, rather peremptorily.

Jordan looked into Sharon's dark brown eyes and just stared, and for reasons which he was never to understand he reached into his pocket and took out a Toonie and tossed it into the air: "Heads I stay, tails I don't."

It landed tails, and Jordan stood up, put the Toonie back into his pocket, and said to Sharon, "I'm married, and I have two beautiful children. I don't know what I'm doing here. I'm sorry, Sharon; I have to go home. My kids are waiting for me. We're having a barbeque..."

♥

OTHER BOOKS BY OREST STOCCO

The Lion that Swallowed Hemingway

Do We Have An Immortal Soul?

Stupidity Is Not a Gift of God
Spiritual Musings – Volume 3

Tea with Grace
A Story of Synchronicity and Platonic Love

Letters to Padre Pio

Jesus Wears Dockers
The Gospel Conspiracy Story

Old Whore Life
Exploring the Shadow Side of Karma

Healing with Padre Pio

Why Bother?
The Riddle of the Good Samaritan

Just Going With the Flow
And Other Spiritual Musings

Keeper of the Flame

My Unborn Child

What Would I Say Today If I Were To Die Tomorrow?
Reflections on the Life of a Seeker

On the Wings of Habitat
A Volunteer's Story

About the Author

Orest Stocco was born in Panettieri, Calabria, Italy. He immigrated to Canada and studied philosophy at university. A student of Gurdjieff's teaching for many years which opened him up to the Way, his passion for writing inspired such works as *The Lion that Swallowed Hemingway* and *Healing with Padre Pio*. He lives in Georgian Bay, Ontario with his life mate Penny Lynn Cates. His personal dictum is: life is an individual journey. Visit him at: http://ostocco.wix.com/ostocco
Spiritual Musings Blog:
http://www.spiritualmusingsbyoreststocco.blogspot.com

ME AND MY SISPHYEAN ROCK

www.ingramcontent.com/pod-product-compliance
Lightning Source LLC
Chambersburg PA
CBHW050748250626
47155CB00005B/1974